HARD TIMES
The Lost Diary of Mrs. Charles Dickens

HARD TIMES
The Lost Diary of Mrs. Charles Dickens

being portions of a journal kept by
Catherine Dickens during her visit to
America in 1842 with her husband

Daniel Panger, B.D., M.Div., editor

CREATIVE ARTS BOOK COMPANY
Berkeley • California • 2000

Hard Times is published by
Donald S. Ellis and distributed by
Creative Arts Book Company

For information contact:
Creative Arts Book Company
833 Bancroft Way
Berkeley, California 94710

ISBN 0-88739-358-6
Library of Congress Catalog Number 00-103043

Printed in the United States of America

Dedicated to Judith Linfield
in loving memory
from her uncle

Introduction

During my year long stay in Godalming, Surrey, a smallish English town, where I served the handful of local Unitarians as their minister, I chanced to discover a boarded up baptistry used a hundred and fifty years earlier when the little chapel had not yet evolved into Unitarianism and was still Anabaptist.

The chapel having been built during the early years of the reign of George III it was not old enough to be of significant historical interest in this nation where scores, if not hundreds of buildings date back to the days of good Queen Bess. And it being an unadorned simple structure, weather-beaten and set back a couple of hundred feet from Meadrow (the old Portsmouth Road) behind an old cemetery containing the remains of undistinguished 19th Century locals, even the townspeople of Godalming paid it little attention. Now in all likelihood three quarters of the ten thousand who live in this district do not even know of its existence.

Being a Californian where anything built prior to the second World War is viewed as ancient, I was fascinated with the old chapel and during the course of a minute examination, prying up some worn linoleum in the area now used to prepare the two dozen cups of tea when the Sunday service was over, I discovered this trapdoor whose handmade square nails I carefully removed. And there below me was the Baptistry. Its dimensions perhaps four feet by six and dreadfully musty smelling with tied up bundles of papers protected by swaths of oilskin piled up on the stone bottom which was some five feet deep. Fully intending to inform the trustees of the congregation about my discovery, yet intensely curious, I carted the bundles up to my room and spent the next five hours carefully untying them and sorting out their contents. As might be expected most of it consisted of old records of the congregation: ledgers, minutes of meetings, membership rolls, records of births, marriages and deaths. But there was one heavy volume of tooled leather, cracked and green with age which was secured by a leather flap with a brass locking mechanism.

Using drops of light machine oil, an ice pick and a nail, after some struggle I managed to open the volume and discovered it to be a journal. And what a journal it turned out to be. The National Trust getting word of it somehow, demanded that I turn it over forthwith, warning me to absolute secrecy so that the curators at the British Museum would have a chance to study it and decide whether to make its existence public or place it in the special archives deeming the contents private and thus inappropriate for any but the highly specialized eyes of one or two historical experts. This determination might take a score or more years to reach, there being no hurry.

Having no choice other than to turn the journal over to the representative of the National Trust who visited me the following week, I did so. But in the five days it was in my possession, I made a careful copy of it which I have kept to myself for the past twenty-five years. But now the National Trust having had sufficient time, yet hearing not a word about this journal of Catherine Dickens kept while she and her husband Charles visited America, I have decided to offer a carefully edited considerable portion of it for publication. Let the National Trust and/or the British Museum do to me what they will (which cannot be too much, I being a citizen and currently a resident of the United States.)

HARD TIMES
The Lost Diary of Mrs. Charles Dickens

HARD TIMES
The Lost Diary of
Mrs. Charles Dickens

ALTHOUGH I EXPRESSED my heartfelt gratitude to dear Daniel Maclise when he presented me with this beautifully bound journal in which to record thoughts and observations during my trip with Mr. Dickens to America, I find I am suffering some moderate trepidation as I open its tooled leather cover and put pen to paper. As is generally known, in spite of my being the loyal and loving wife of one of the world's most gifted authors, I am, at best, just a middling scribbler who must labour over every sentence and even after my best efforts, am rarely satisfied with my accomplishment. Had it not been for my anticipation of Mr. Maclise's disappointment should I report that his gift remained unused, I doubt that I would even consider attempting this record—doubtless the shadow of Mr. Dickens' genius has had its effect. But to disappoint a friend, such as Daniel Maclise has been to my family, would lay so heavily on me that I have forced myself to overcome my reluctance. One thing I can gain comfort from as I invade

1

the pristine beauty of these smooth vellum sheets is that no one's eyes, other than my own, will ever have a chance to peruse my jottings until at least one hundred years after my death. By then it will hardly matter, for not only will my children all be gone to a better world, but in all likelihood their children as well. So with the firm intention to secure this journal as stated above I commence:

Monday, the seventeenth, January 1842, Banks of Newfoundland.

Mr. Dickens being busily engaged in a flurry of letter writing, the ocean at last sufficiently calm that my bouts of nausea are at least under control, I can state without much fear of ever having to make any corrections that the past fourteen days have been the most miserable of my life. So much so that there were times not only did I despair of surviving, I fervently wished that the end would come. And the sooner the better.

From almost the first moment the S.S. Brittania departed from Liverpool, the fourth day of this month, I have been overwhelmed with seasickness. Of course I have heard accounts of travelers of our acquaintance who suffered from this malady during ocean voyages. But never in my most distraught imaginings did I have any true concept of the severity of this condition and how completely it can rack the body of any human being subject to its full impact. That my maid Annie was untouched by this malady and was able to care for me was my only salvation. Now Mr. Dickens whose normal vitality and his excitement at the prospect of this trip (unlike my deepening apprehension) I fully expected to weather the tossings and plungings of this vessel with but little effect, as did he, was, alas, as it turned out, a companion in my sickness. At times possibly even more miserable for he viewed this as a weakness and was ashamed, although after the worst of the storms he was back on his feet while I still fancied myself to be among the dying. To be fair to my husband, to whom his vitality is a matter of such pride (not one of his friends, not Forster, not Macready, not Minton could keep up with him on one of his fast multimile walks) I must state that the operation to repair his fistula shortly before we left England had laid him low (the pain was not to be described in spite of liberal quantities of opium) so that he spent entire days stretched out on the divan, pale as death and unable to repress an occasional moan even when the children were present.

Ah, the children. Just mentioning them feels like the nib of this pen has entered my heart. How could I have left my darlings? Will I ever see Charley, Marmey, Katey, and Baby Walter again? Of course I will. What a silly goose I am as

Mr. Dickens is wont to say when I am in one of my woe-is-me funks. But the real heartbreak is how are the four of them taking the separation. Certainly you will never find a more loving and more responsible couple than the Macreadys. But can there ever be an adequate substitute for one's mother? And, yes, for one's father? Especially when the father is as doting and willing to get down on all fours to play as is my very dear husband. Yet, as I think about it, Charles does not appear to be a tenth part as concerned about leaving the children and undertaking this jaunt to a distant land as do I. From the way he hovers over them when they fall sick and his spoiling them with sweetmeats and presents, I would have thought differently. If he has shed a tear at their absence, I have not seen it. And I have shed buckets. In fact, right now while my cheeks are wet and my eyes swollen and red from the pain of separation, he is planning some sort of testimonial to honor John Hewett, captain of our ship, and is strolling up and down arm in arm with the Earl of Mulgrave with whom he has become fast friends during the course of this trip. With a certainty, my husband Charles is one who knows how to make friends. Not that he does not already have more than an ample supply. In fact, I am willing to admit (but only in this private journal) that there are times I find myself growing jealous at the intensity and intimacy of his relationships and

I can't help feeling that in ways he is closer to John Forster and several others than he is to me. Perhaps if I shared his ability to make friends with those of my own sex and could go off for ten mile walks with them and stay up til all hours offering toasts and having a rollicking good time, I would feel less jealous. Oh well, I guess that is a portion of the price I must pay for having been joined for life with a man like my husband. As they say, genius makes its own way and it is the duty of a wife to go along with her husband come what may. Well, perhaps that's not exactly what they say, but it sounds about right.

Twentieth January:

The past two days have been simply dreadful. When I made my previous entry in this journal, I had every reason to expect that the worst of this nightmare journey was over. After all, had we not finally reached the shores of the New World after that tumultuous crossing? But relief for my poor body was not to be as we sailed south along the coast to Halifax Harbour. Now, not only was my stomach stirred up so that I was unable to retain anything more than tiny sips of water, but my face swole so that I looked more a pumpkin than a human being. Needless to say, I secured myself against the gaze of others in our cabin and turned my face

to the wall when Mr. Dickens entered knowing full well
how much my condition upset and disgusted him. Yes, disgusted is the word. At heart he is as sensitive as a child
when the appearance of his helpmeet is distorted as it frequently is when I suffer any sort of indisposition even those
that members of my sex are forced to bear at each cycle of
the moon. Although I would die before I would breathe a
word of this to him, I have gained the impression that the,
alas, all too often condition of my face is reflected in the features of certain of his fictional characters. The first example
of this was the "fat boy" in Pickwick Papers. And I must
confess to closeting myself for half a day after my introduction to that unsettling creature so profuse were tears I was
unable to control.

Despite this painful indisposition of mine, commencing
shortly after we left the Banks of Newfoundland, other than
polite inquiries as to how I did, Mr. Dickens, who was once
again his robust self, paid little attention to me investing
most of his time in either thickening his friendship with the
Earl of Mulgrave or in writing letters, principally to John
Forster. Three thousand miles of ocean away, yet Forster's
presence is as much with us as when just a few miles of road
separated and he could drop in, unannounced, any time he
pleased. Perhaps it is the residue of my indisposition that
causes me to say this (my face is still painfully pumpkin-

like) but I believe Mr. D. loves Forster more than he does his own poor wife. Now I suppose I should be grateful to "Sir" John for all the effort he has expended on helping Mr. D. shape and polish his literary productions. And who am I to say that even without his dearest friend's assistance he would have achieved as much literary success as he has with it. I must leave such conclusions to those far more learned than I. Yet it is I who am forced to suffer in silence Forster's poorly concealed patronization. In his eyes, I am little more than a fixture around the house useful for getting tea, at times ornamental, but never of any true significance in the astonishing manifestations of Mr. D.'s genius. He on the other hand. . . .Yet it may be said of Mr. D. that in his heart and, alas all too often in his behavior, he shares "Sir" John's perceptions. But added to my getting tea and my ornamental usefulness is my availability as a receptacle for my husband's undiminished amorous nature.

Having reviewed the above paragraphs, it behooves me to say that whatever lacks there may be in Mr. Dickens' relationship with me, they are more than compensated for by his concern for the abused and unfortunate of our species whose plight he attempts to redress in his novels. And, closer to home, his increasing affection and limitless patience with his children who adore him and who, at this moment, must be heartbroken at his absence and the prospect of it continuing for some time. Oh why did I agree to accompanying him on this dreadful trip?" If I were home instead of tossing aboard this foul smelling ship off the coast of a land inhabited principally by red savages, I could comfort my babies and murmur reassurances that their daddy would return in good time, and despite his distance, still loves and adores them. Why, oh why did I agree to go along!

Tremont House, (Boston), Saturday, twenty-second January, 1842.

Not in my wildest imaginings did I ever envision anything even remotely resembling that which took place upon our arrival at the American city of Boston. Of course I had a premonition that something extraordinary was about to happen when at least a dozen men with newspapers under their arms came leaping aboard our ship, risking their lives even before we were moored to the wharf. And these were no news boys, rather editors of the various newspapers: editors themselves! with no other purpose than to interview Mr. Dickens, each striving to get the beat on the others. Then, when we disembarked and made our way by carriage through the streets of the city with crowds lining the sidewalks shouting and waving their hats, with masses of men and women pouring into the street surrounding the carriage so that our progress was at a snail's pace—the noise and confusion beyond belief—Victoria herself should she ever venture to this foreign land could not anticipate a reception greater than that afforded my dear Charles. "Beyond belief," those were his very words when we finally settled in our rooms after a banquet of a luncheon, someone or other had prepared for us where every bite of food was accompanied by one local dignitary or another coming over to shake the hand that penned Oliver Twist, Nicholas Nickleby and all the rest.

Despite all the hoopla and confusion of our triumphal pilgrimage from shipside to hotel, I did make it my business to focus whatever attention was possible on the passing scene and it is my impression that Boston need not suffer in comparison to one of our lesser cities. Bath comes to mind, possible Portsmouth because of its coastal location. A nice tidy town, but one that would not expect to make more than a minor impression on anyone who has known the magnificence, dignity and, yes, culture of London. From certain offhand remarks and, now and again, a fleeting facial expression, I think Mr. Dickens' impression of Boston was not unlike my own. In a word, a town that thought itself more than it is by a good measured mile and one that would take instant umbrage at anyone so incautious as to so much as hint at such a thing.

Fremont Hotel, Tuesday, twenty-fifth January— half an hour to midnight.

Exhaustion, headaches and a never-ending swirl of activities, events, visits and visitors have kept me from my journal since Saturday. But thank God for the kind ministrations of my dear Annie without whom I believe I would perish. To cap this swirl of activity off was the event of this evening. To wit: a public dinner to honor Boz at three pounds sterling a ticket. Three pounds sterling! A week's wages for a skilled journeyman, a good month's for a servant. I was shocked, but of course said nothing. Mr. D. professed to be shocked, but I could see a twinkle in his eye that declared charging the public such a sum to be in the presence of "His Greatness" was not exactly displeasing. Well, so be it. If anyone has earned the right to be so honoured it is my beloved husband. Some say his books, in their way, have sparked a bloodless revolution in England. That Parliament and even the prime Minister are responsive to such as Nicholas Nickleby. It would be callow of me not to confess that I am warmed by the honours steeped upon my husband. After all no one is closer or knows him better and there can be little doubt things with him would have been quite different were I not his wife. Yet it would be nice if, on occasion, I received some small recognition for the role I have played these many years, not excluding a listening ear particularly during the birth pangs of each of his novels in turn when even John Forster must wait til the work is well underway. It would be comforting if the press, in addition to the briefest of mentions that I too was present with perhaps a word or two about my gown and my hairstyle, would offer just a suggestion of a hint that a wife's role is not without significance in the lives of great men. Now I am not one much given to being critical of Mr. Dickens—to his face never. But that florid waistcoat he wore to the banquet of which he is inordinately proud might be acceptable, on occasion, in such a cosmopolitan place as London, but here in staid Boston: my goodness! Perhaps, had he observed my expression as I watched him put it on, he would have thought better of it. But he didn't And thus he entered the banquet hall giving the initial impression of a Roman candle fully fired up.

Four hours past midnight, twenty sixth January.

Thinking him asleep, I busied myself with the above entry but shortly after a nearby church struck midnight, Mr. Dickens suddenly sat bolt upright in bed and commenced staring at a free standing closet with a lion's head brass handle onto which is affixed a full length mirror as if, at any moment, he expected it to come alive. After surely fifteen minutes of this during which I three times cleared my throat, he launched into what proved to be a conversation with himself although for the first few seconds his words were directed to me. But then his attention shifted back to the closet mirror. Much of what he said, I failed to understand although I tried. A more educated person than I might have done better. But the effort to understand, copyrights was what he was going on about, was so irritating and had such a depressing effect as I was forced to face my educational defects, it reached a point that either he stopped talking or I was in danger of losing my mind. So, to protect my sanity, I started to show evidence of amourous feeling, although truthfully I was very little inclined in that direction, which caused this one sided conversation to end as Mr. Dickens started responding.

It is not generally known, perhaps; only to me, but Mr. Dickens is a very amourous man. Yet his approaches to me have always been in the dark. But this time the lights were not immediately extinguished and during the short time before they were, my husband's hand wearing the ring of Mary, my dead sister, came into view and the sight of that ring brought on a numbness and a fervent wish that somehow I could be transported three thousand miles from here and once again be in the midst of my poor babies while Mr.

Dickens continued on with his American business without the burden of an unhappy and homesick wife. If comforting was what he needed while I was no longer with him, from the reaction of the female portion of those attending the banquet, there were at least fifty members of my sex present who would not have been adverse to bestowing their favours on him. Perhaps a better person than I, or should I say a stronger person, would not have suffered such a numbing reaction at the sight of my dear dead sister's ring on my husband's hand as he embraced me. But I freely confess my weakness. And I also confess to a feeling of shame at my jealous reaction to one who, by now, has mouldered to little more than dust in her grave. I entertain not the slightest suspicion as to Mary's innocence in her relationship to Mr. Dickens. Although the affection he openly bestowed on her far exceeded that which was mine. Of all the creatures of the world there were none more chaste or trusting than my long departed sister. And at the very most Mr. Dickens' lips may have brushed her cheeks, but only on rare occasions; although they frequently walked hand in hand through the garden and across the fields with Mr. Dickens chatting away and Mary dutifully listening. And for this I suffered searing pangs of jealousy! For shame, Kate. And still, with all the years which have passed since her short life of seventeen years came to an end, jealousy gnaws at your heart and lungs at the sight of the ring he took from her dead hand and placed on his finger the night of her death. For shame.

Sleep having overcome Mr. Dickens, as is always the case after an amorous episode, I relit the bedside lamp which had finally been extinguished and directed my gaze to my husband's face. There could be no doubt he was a handsome man with his face, now in repose, framed by his soft, wavy, chestnut hair. Despite all the years that have passed, he looked no older than the day I first met him, sleep having eased away the lines of care. And that smooth high forehead of his, what yet untapped heights of genius it contained. Scarcely a third of the way into his fourth decade and already established as one of the leading literary figures of the world, if not the most revered. Witness that reception upon his arrival in this distant land and the tumultuous events since. How dare I allow petty jealousy, a jealousy directed toward one long gone, sully what must be considered one of the most enviable marriages anywhere on this earth. Rather than this base emotion, I should honour my husband for preserving the memory of my sister by wearing her ring day and night, year in and year out since her death.

Fremont Hotel, Boston twenty-eighth January, Friday, 1842.

That I have managed to find time to return to my journal toward which I am experiencing increasing affection, must be counted as a miracle. Such a swirl of activity has surrounded Mr. Dickens and myself, I have lost track of the sequence of events. Faces and names have become scrambled in my brain. Half the time I do not know if it is yesterday or tomorrow and my exhaustion exceeds anything I have ever known. That I have not been prostrated by some disease or other must be counted as one of the wonders of the age. From the moment Mr. Dickens and I leave our rooms we are surrounded by hundreds, thousands more when we exit the hotel and these constantly coughing, spitting, sneezing and exhibiting in a hundred other ways their infectious maladies which back home common decency would have restrained them from leaving the privacy of their homes. Truthfully, although I am the more delicate, most of my concern has been for Mr. Dickens. For hands in every stage of cleanliness or lack of same are constantly grabbing his hand which he is forced to soak in warm water several times a day to reduce the swelling and relieve the tenderness and those whose coughing is most severe are the ones who, by the use of their elbows, come up closer to us and think nothing of pushing their inflamed faces to within inches of his. Even in the privacy of our rooms, there is no relief. Let us open the door for the briefest moment to allow a waiter to deliver some refreshments and a score of clamouring men and women will invade us. Every sort of subterfuge has been used to gain entrance to the great man including forged letters of introduction from acquaintances of his.

Of course among these hordes of invaders there has also been a sprinkling of the great and near great. We have spent time with Richard Henry Dana, he of "Two Years Before the Mast" which I devoured not long since; the poet Henry Wadsworth Longfellow; one John, I believe Bigelow, secretary of the Commonwealth; a Mister Quincy, President of the Senate, and of course, others better known to Mr.. Dickens than to myself. Now Mr. Dana, although appearing somewhat fatigued or perhaps unwell, is a very handsome man and having so recently immersed myself in his book, I could not help but feel a certain attachment to him and thoroughly enjoyed the short time we spent together. Longfellow, on the other hand, despite the reported excellence of his poetry, I found to be rather stuffy and from his general manner one could almost say he was engaged in having a love affair with himself. Perhaps I am being catty. But no matter. This journal is for my eyes alone so I will say what I please.

One event that I must record here is a dramatization of Nicholas Nickleby written and directed by Joe Field, a well known local comedian. It took place at the Tremont Theatre and as we entered and took our seats, the orchestra played the "Boz Waltzes," especially composed for this occasion, and the audience cheered nine or ten times delaying by a good quarter of an hour the commencement of the production, which for some reason which escapes me was entitled, "Charles O'Malley."

Then as a dessert to this enjoyable feast—Mr. Dickens was all smiles during the entire production—Mr. Fields offered an entertainment entitled, "Boz, a Masquerade Phrenologic." This skit, to my husband's shouted delight, contained a sly hint at the way American writers, no less than foreign, are injured by the lack of an international copyright agreement. So enthusiastic was Mr. Dickens at this, that he rushed backstage after the performance and embraced Mr. Fields who dissolved into tears at this display of emotion. Oh how the copyright issue burns in my husband's breast and I cannot help but have misgivings about how this passion of his may affect our visit. For his works, although widely known in this nation, have produced precious little income for us thus far with little prospect for any improvement.

Second, February, Wednesday.

Two events stand out since my last entry into this journal. A banquet of gargantuan proportions in my husband's honour and a chance meeting with one who I last laid eyes upon some sixteen or seventeen years ago. I shall deal with the second mentioned first.

I was strolling about Boston Common, accompanied by a young chap named George W. Putnam, recently hired by Mr. Dickens as his personal secretary for the duration of our stay in America. Ten dollars a month and board was the rather modest sum agreed upon. (But of course being in the intimate company of an author of Mr. Dickens' stature might be viewed as sufficient payment in itself.) We had circled the Common once and were commencing our second circle (I had been feeling unwell and the brisk air was doing me good) when I heard someone call out in a cultured female voice, "Kate Hogarth—is that you?" I turned and immediately to my left was a stylishly dressed, perhaps a little overweight woman, who I judged to be in her early thirties, hand in hand with a lanky girl, rather sullen faced, who reminded me of one of my schoolmates with whom I was moderately friendly some twenty years earlier. It took me several moments to realize that, in fact, the stylishly dressed woman was herself my friend of two decades past and three thousand miles distant from the grassy knoll behind the schoolhouse where we played together and endlessly talked about: when we were older and the young men who would come calling.

"Rebecca Simmons," I said extending my hand which she took and held tightly. "Becky Simmons, my goodness, I am simply thunderstruck."

"As am I," she said, "as am I," and we embraced as her sullen faced daughter shuffled to one side and stared vacantly at Mr. Putnam's shoes. "What are you doing here in Boston?" she said.

"I might ask the same question," I said laughing.

"Oh, my husband and I immigrated right after our marriage years ago. He had a brother here in the city in the banking business who needed a partner. But you, Kate—what a surprise."

"I am here with Mr. Dickens—he insisted I join him for a tour of America."

"Mr. Dickens?" She had a puzzled expression on her face. "Mr. Charles Dickens, the author," I nodded. She sucked in her breath. "Kate, I am shocked. :You are traveling as a companion to Charles Dickens!" She looked horrified.

"Hardly a companion," I laughed. He is my husband and the father of my four wonderful children."

"Husband. . .father of. . ." She plunged her hand into her reticule and pulled out a bottle salts which she brought to her nose, drew in several mighty sniffs, then pressed the back of her gloved hand to her forehead. Finally she managed to say, "I had no idea—hadn't heard a thing. After we lost touch with one another and then my crossing the Atlantic. . . .And to think I've read every one of your husband's novels and laughed and cried a dozen times with each and never knew. . . .Well, I suppose stranger things have happened. But not to me." She took another sniff of her salts.

My reaction to all this at first was disbelief. How could she not know—how could anyone not know? But that disbelief was quickly replaced with a sinking of my spirits. Her reaction had been too genuine; her surprise too great—her face had actually gone pale. She knew nothing of Mr. Dickens' wife. And without a doubt tens of thousands, hundreds of thousands of his avid readers know nothing, will never know. I could travel the length and breadth of England, to say nothing of America, and unless I use the name Mrs.. Charles Dickens, I will be viewed has just another middle aged woman on holiday, of interest only for the few shillings she might be willing to part with.

"If I had known, Kate, if I had only known how exciting it would have all been. We could have corresponded. I could have offered you and your husband hospitality in our lovely home." She smiled and her eyes twinkled. "And what jealousy I could have generated amongst my friends, all of whom are devoted admirers of Mr. Dickens as is almost the entire literate population of this city."

Despite a heaviness I felt and the return of a throbbing headache, I allowed this girlhood friend to take my arm and propel me forward while her now wide-eyed daughter, open-mouthed after hearing our exchange, trailed behind with poor Mr. Putnam, whom I failed to introduce, his hands deep in his trouser pockets taking up the rear.

"I still can't get over it," she said in a familiar way as if only days had passed since our last meeting instead of years. "Imagine Kate Hogarth and Charles Dickens who has turned this town upside down since his arrival. Well, this world is filled with wonders and you certainly are one of them, dearest Kate." Then taking a deep breath and holding it a moment, which I remembered was a habit of hers back when we were girls, she launched into a detailed account of her life here in Boston, exhibiting no modesty about her place in society.

Although from her account, confirmed by the quality of her outfit which included several unquestionably valuable pieces of jewelry that her condition of life was one only great wealth could provide, certainly far in excess of that which I and Mr. Dickens enjoyed, I gained the impression that she was not a happy person and our chance meeting had caused her not a little distress she was unable to effectively mask by her smiles, laughter, and chatter as she walked me around the Common, once, twice, thrice with apparently no concern for her daughter who had again turned sullen and was mumbling to herself and scuffling her feet. Poor Mr. Putnam, good natured chap that he was, dutifully followed without sighs or throat-clearings so that I determined to suggest to Mr. Dickens that ten dollars a month was a bit on the skimpy side, three dollars a week or ten shillings being more appropriate.

It was on our third circumnavigation of that now quite familiar open space that Becky Simmons, now Mrs. Joshua Adams, broke off from her account of her present existence and, pulling me to a halt and looking me directly in the eye asked, "How does he do it—your husband; those books of his?" From the suddenness and manner of the question, it was as if it had been on her mind ever since she had discovered my relationship to him and had finally burst forth.

Now I have asked that question of myself any number of times starting with the appearance of Samuel Weller in Pickwick whose various antics had caused me to laugh so hard my stomach ached. There were times, especially when I read aloud to my sisters, that my mirth was so great tears filled my eyes and the words swam away as laughter choked me. But my response to Becky was a polite raising of my eyebrows and something about genius having a mysterious source of its own. And then, pleading fatigue and a splitting headache and offering as an excuse for not accepting an invitation to her "lovely home," our imminent departure from Boston, we parted and I returned to the hotel leaning rather heavily upon Mr. Putnam's arm for I had not been fabricating when I mentioned that headache and fatigue. Mr. Dickens was off, I believe to Harvard College which he persisted in calling Cambridge University because of its location in Cambridge Towne. Then, stretched out on my bed, my mind churned with thoughts of my long lost youth, generated by that amazing chance meeting with Becky. But finally the question Becky had asked, "How does he do it?" took command of my thinking.

Unlike past times when I wondered about the genius of the man I had married and finally mentally threw up my hands with a sense that it all was beyond me, this time I forced myself to stick with it. Meeting Becky and the emotions this generated had something to do with it. But now for the first time in years actually having time to think, without babies and the household chores darting in and out of my consciousness, probably played an even more important role in this exercise of mental discipline. And, yes, being with my husband for far longer periods of time than was usual and sharing this adventure with him also played a part.

Who was this man I shared a bed with who could excite an entire city into a form of adulation-generated madness? Crowds had swirled around him wherever he went. People forced their way into our rooms who were perfect strangers. Scores, if not hundreds of messages arrived daily, each more urgent than the other. But behind all this was that flood of literary works whose combined words, by now, surely exceeds three million and he yet a young man with every prospect of living another three or four decades. I thought of the way he had stared at the standing closet here in our room, I mentioned earlier in this journal. He was more than looking at its full length mirror and lion head brass knob, he was absorbing it. Never have I known, or even heard of anyone with the power of concentration enjoyed by Mr. Dickens. He was able to write with children and servants coming and going—even with workmen in the house sawing and hammering; write with no letup page after page in an atmosphere which often drove me frantic. I turned my thoughts to his most recent work whose little Nell on her deathbed had caused half of England to dissolve into tears, myself included. What a marvelous combination of pathos and humour that novel contained. I reviewed in my mind the procession of characters that marched through, "The Old Curiosity Shop," characters possibly more familiar to me than to anyone else on earth excepting Mr. Dickens himself. For hadn't I, time and again, been exposed to passages he earnestly read to me in the privacy of our bedroom, then a night or two later these same passages revised and invariably improved. I was as familiar with Dick Swivler, Samson Brass, Daniel Quilp as I was with neighbours of ours who lived in adjoining houses. I found myself whispering their names, artful names as are those given to most of his characters. Then I found myself repeating the name of the hideous dwarf Daniel Quilp, terrifying and strong as a lion though scarcely four and a half feet in height. And at that moment, from the recesses of my memory, I remembered mentioning to Mr. Dickens, five or six years ago, that I had watched a man at least a head shorter than myself wrestling barrels of beer off a wagon and, that I had been struck by his strength and his ugliness which together produced a quite unsettling effect in me. Mr. Dickens had asked me about the man's arms and hands, about the width of his shoulders. Other things. Til this moment I'd forgotten our conversation. Yet I was virtually certain that from our exchange Daniel Quilp had sprung four or five years later. Mr. Dickens absorbed everything. Nothing was lost. His mind, apparently, was a limitless storehouse from which he could pick and choose. Of course Quilp, as must be true of all of his characters, was more than what he gained from me. Thousands of conversations and images were there in his mind to enable him to flesh out his characters. As little Nell wasn't just my sister Mary, my husband's one time chaste love, anymore than Quilp was that pitiful fellow I saw wrestling beer barrels off that wagon. Forgetting the illustrations by Cattermole and Phiz, if I should chance to meet poor little Nell emerging from the actual old Curiosity Shop I would not recognize her as my sister Mary. For even to her Mr. Dickens, the artist he is, added bits and pieces from others in his storehouse shaping it all into something new.

All of this, in part, was in answer to Becky's "How does he do it?" Although lying there on my bed, my headache gone and more relaxed than I had been any time since commencing this journey, I had a powerful awareness that there was still much more to the answer to her question. That, as certain critics had begun to say, Mr. Dickens is a force of nature and as such there may be parts of him, of his genius, that are beyond comprehension.

Well, I have certainly waxed long, if not eloquent, about Becky Simmons and the aftereffects of our meeting. As to the other event that took place today deserving of inclusion in this journal, just a few lines.

No more than two or three times in my life have I attended such a banquet as that held at Papanti's honoring Mr. Dickens. A choice of more than forty items on the menu was offered to the hundred who had paid fifteen dollars for the privilege of dining with and toasting my husband. The most prominent of those present and these included almost everyone of substance here in Boston proposing the toasts. Would that Mr. Dickens had so much as hinted to me what he intended to say in response to the affection and praise heaped upon him. Had I had but an inkling, I would have done everything in my power to dissuade him; the good Lord only knows if that would have caused him to modify what he said. As it was, in addition to fulsome appreciation for all that had been said, he referred, thankfully briefly, to the copyright issue and how unfair it was to authors not to have the protection of an international agreement. Thus, in a scant five minutes, he eroded a significant portion of the good will he had accumulated. And I overheard mutterings about what he said being in bad taste, he being a guest of this nation and the recipient of so much lavish hospitality. I shuddered to think what tomorrow's newspapers would have to say for I recognized several editors madly scribbling in their notebooks with unmistakably sour expressions on their faces. And today's newspapers, as I was certain they would, screamed that he had been guilty of bad taste and had been responsible for considerable dissonance amoung the ranks of those gathered to honour him. Need I state, I do not dare to utter so much as a single word to Mr. Dickens regarding this matter. For after reading the comments in several newspapers he glowered and looked as if he would bite the head off anyone who dared mention the matter.

Sixth, February, Saturday

As is generally known, train travel is difficult for me. Even relatively short trips have their effect and every time I am forced to board one of these evil-smelling smoke and fire belching monsters, my principal feeling is regret that this method of travel had ever been invented. I would rather by a hundred times go by coach, gladly investing the extra hours that mode of transportation requires. Being able to breathe pure air far outweighs getting from one place to another lickety split. Yet so many others, Mr. Dickens amongst them, think otherwise. The upshot of our trip to Wooster was my face swelling to twice its normal size and a general feeling of distress that, no matter how I struggled against it, brought thoughts of impending death or at the very least general paralysis. And Mr. Dickens was hard pressed to conceal his annoyance as if I had somehow deliberately brought this condition on myself.

For the past several hours I have been closeted in our room in the home of the honourable Governor Davis, a comfortable enough room and the hospitality has been adequate. But a quarter of an hour ago I grew so desperate I turned to this journal for relief. Although it pains me to say, I am of the opinion that Mr. Dickens actually welcomes these episodes of mine that cause me to confine myself to my room. With me out of the way he's free to be as flirtatious as he wishes and it frees him to engage him in strutting about in that devil-may-care manner my presence often inhibits. So why, I ask, did he insist on my accompanying him on this trip to America? Without the burden of my presence there would be no limit to how he might choose to act up, and the flirtations: limitless. I suppose the answer is, I am useful to him when the day is over and he retires to his room; and I do not refer exclusively to those needs stimulated by his amorous nature. Time and again he has used me as a foil for one or another of his ideas. I am the first one with whom he shares his observations. How many nights I forced myself to stay awake while he went on and on about whatever happened to be invading his mind at the moment. And those times when he is disappointed or annoyed or frustrated by some difficulty in a project he's engaged in, it is always Kate who he turns to first. Not for advice, certainly not. That is the province of the likes of John Forster. It is a listening ear which I provide. Time and again he has worked himself out of a funk or solved some problem by the simple expedience of talking at me. Yes, that is the more accurate description. Of course, there have been times when I risked the wrath of my lord and master by offering an opinion or a comment not in line with his point of view. Rarely has he reacted at the moment when I ventured my head into lion's mouth. But for several days after he is wont to exhibit a coldness, bordering on indifference, I find particularly painful. Oh yes, there have been those infrequent times when Charles was plunged into despair and he laid his head on my bosom and wept. Those times what I had to say was listened to and were not without effect. But who would wish their husband to be in such a condition so that their own feelings about themselves might be bolstered? Surely not I.

Regarding the above rather lengthy paragraph, I detect an element of self pity and if charged with it, I must plead guilty. But it is not only since my marriage to Mr. Dickens that elements of my life are deserving of pity—being hidden from the world who other than the one who suffers should provide this pity? My life at home before I met Mr. Dickens, although my father's position guaranteed economic sufficiency, because I was the oldest and unquestionably the strongest, much of the burden of the family rested on my

shoulders. More often than not those functions and responsibilities the province of a mother were transferred to me.
For most of their needs the children came to me not to our
mother. The day to day running of the household was large-
ly in my hands. And my father, whose ways Mr. Dickens
reflects, at least in part, would unburden himself to me but
not with the expectation of a response. And having learned
this early on, I almost never offered more than head nods
and facial expressions declaring unwavering interest. But
unlike Mr. Dickens, my father, on occasion, would pass
along to me for revision or correction a piece from one of
the stringers of the Evening Chronicle of which he was the
editor in chief. Shortly after our marriage when I offered
like services to Mr. Dickens, he smiled and patted me on the
shoulder and said, "Running our household will be quite
enough for you, dear Kate." I never made the offer again.

Well, I find that pouring my heart out has been more
effective than any medicine. So perhaps I will join my husband and his coterie of admirers downstairs—if only I
could free myself of trepidation at the prospect of those
train rides that still await us before we reach New York City
where we will be able to settle in for some time.

Carlton House, New York, twelfth February, Saturday

Finally I have the opportunity to return to my precious journal. Was it only six days ago I last sat down to its welcoming pages? It feels like weeks.

The journey from Governor Davis' house to this bustling city proved considerably less burdensome than I anticipated. Rather than suffering the jostling and stench of train travel, after a short canal boat journey from Springfield to Hartford, thankfully lasting only two hours during which my face swole dreadfully; we boarded a large comfortable boat and coasted down Long Island Sound, with scarcely a ripple disturbing its tranquil waters. At New Haven, where we put up at the Tontine Hotel, Mr. Dickens was serenaded by Yale students who must have numbered close to a thousand, and, as was to be expected, crowds milled around the hotel and it took the efforts of two stout porters, locking hands across the main stairway, to keep portions of this crowd from swarming into the reception room. As it was, a stream of visitors came and went, shaking poor Charles' hand til it was painfully swollen. And the flow only came to a halt about 11:00 o'clock when we finally were able to stagger to our rooms where he and I collapsed. Yet our exhaustion was such, it took us upwards of an hour before we enjoyed the relief of sleep.

Unlike Boston, which resembles one of England's lesser yet lovely cities, New York, although probably only half the size of London, can be compared to England's reigning city in both its ugliness and magnificence: slums that matched those of Cheapside and spires and steeples together with magnificent houses fit for belted earls. But I doubt if there is a single hotel in all of London the equal of the Carlton House. Splendid is the only word that adequately describes our suite of rooms. Both Mr. Dickens and I shuddered at what must be the cost. Almost certainly it would exceed that of the Fremont in Boston whose bill proved to be simply shocking, although the management assured us that it had received a substantial discount in honour of Mr. Dickens' reputation and the increased income the hotel enjoyed during his stay. Well, both Mr. D. and I knew that this trip would be costly. And I have no doubt that a book or two, to say nothing of a flurry of articles, are already in the process of gestation and upon our return to England will help to offset this cost.

Although I had been much restored by the tranquil boat trip, my face, alas, was still dreadfully swollen when we reached the city and I kept it hidden as best I could with veil and scarf and I would not be surprised if I were taken for one recently recovered from the pox as we entered the hotel, muffled as I was.

As was inevitable, just as Mr. Dickens and I were sitting down to dinner, my face still partially hidden by a veil despite his poo-pooing my vanity, America's most famous author, Washington Irving, came in with open arms and he and Mr. Dickens embraced and then he must buss me on the cheek and it all proved very trying and I excused myself after only nibbling at the bountiful plate of appetizers the hotel management had presented as a gift. Of course I had read with considerable delight Mr. Irving's Knickerbocher Tales and I knew in what high regard Mr. Dickens held him. But had I not excused myself when I did, embarrassment, combined with my being in a delicate part of the month, would have almost certainly caused me to faint dead away. Now with sips of wine and my dear journal in hand, I am, if not a new person, at least one who has been somewhat patched back together.

Seeing Mr. Irving and thinking about *The Legend of Sleepy Hollow* and other of his delightful tales, I cannot help but wonder how Mr. D. will shape the material stored in his brain during the course of this trip into those literary efforts he will undertake upon our return to England. Watching his head swivel and his eyes dart as we rode up Broadway from the Battery to this hotel, I knew the wheels of his mind were racing. And that as soon as he had the chance, he would be here, there and everywhere in this city, not missing a thing, including prisons, hospitals, orphan homes and the places where the old and infirm congregate waiting for the end.

Now I would never even breathe a word of this to my closest friend, but I suspect Mr. Dickens' interest in prisons, hospitals and the like is not only a product of his well known crusading nature, but also affords him a carefully concealed satisfaction as he contrasts the lives of the poor wretches confined in those places with the free and eventful life fortune has bestowed upon him. Once from Mr. Dickens' mother I heard a chance remark about some difficult time in her son's early life when he was forced to work briefly in the manufacture of the blacking used on boots. Perhaps if this is not one of Mrs. Dickens' imaginings (a habit she is prone to) that experience had its effect on him. So that when he views misery, not only is there that special satisfaction in knowing that for him it is long past and will never return, but also a feeling of compassion for those who still suffer and a determination to do something about it. And, if what Mrs. Dickens said is true, this compassion is the most laudable part of my husband's personality. Alas, all too many people who have known suffering early in their lives and now live comfortably or more than comfortably not only have they no interest in those less fortunate but actively detest and revile them. It has been often said: there is no taskmaster worse than one who himself was at one time ground down. Yet I must ask myself if the blacking factory employment be true, why has Mr. Dickens never said a word about it? Could it be that he is ashamed? If so, what a tragedy. For such an experience does not make him a lesser man, but a greater.

Fifteenth February, Carlton House, Tuesday

Here I am having taken breakfast in bed after what must be the most exhausting evening of my life. Needless to say, Mr. Dickens is up and away and who knows what dark corner of this metropolis he is poking his nose into at the moment. As for me, my poor body aches from that Boz Ball of last night where I marched the ballroom round and round to allow whoever choose to gawk at me, then danced with the Mayor of the city who was not above treading on my toes on occasion. And then, of course, as Mr. Dickens was being greeted by what felt like half the population of the city, I must stand by his side putting on the best face possible (this despite some slight residue of swelling) and offer my hand, nod, or mumble something pleasant as the procession passed by.

The ball took place at Park Theatre. Fortunately we found a way to enter through the stage door. I do not even want to think about what would have transpired had we tried the front entrance around which and stretching away in both directions milled a crowd of several thousand, including a sprinkling of toughs, who might have snatched all in our party naked in an attempt to secure souvenirs. Inside the theatre it was bedlam.

Now there is something about the quality or should I say the manner of people in New York that causes me to think not unkindly of Boston. There, all in all, despite bargings into our rooms on occasion, there was a certain overlay of politeness even consideration. Not so in Knickerbocher town. Although, as requested, Mr. Dickens and I, accompanied by Mayor and Mayoress, paraded twice around that large ballroom, there were hoots and shouts by those who failed to get a close enough glimpse of "his greatness." And when we danced, me with the Mayor, Mr. Dickens with his lady, at times we were bumped into by the more eager and not always was there an "excuse me," instead a look of delight at having made contact, in a manner of speaking, which will, no doubt, be embellished upon when recounted and re-recounted. Perhaps it is indelicate of me to mention, but an odour permeated that ball, which grew more and more offensive by the moment, that could only have come from indifferently and infrequently washed bodies and clothing that had not known the salutary effect of soap and water in a fortnight or longer.

Until we arrived here in New York it never once entered my mind that our dear Queen Victoria was exposed to any sort of suffering and distress. Rather, like any good subject, I admired her and thought of her as one of the most fortunate human beings on earth. But now, having suffered the press of crowds beyond endurance, no matter that this press is a product of adulation, I cannot but sympathize with Her Majesty who experiences the presence of masses of adoring people wherever she goes. But, unlike Her Majesty who is well protected from actual physical contact with these masses and when she so chooses can retreat to the privacy and security of Buckingham Palace where none dare even attempt to follow her, my husband and I are mauled, our hands shaken swollen every time we step out of the hotel. And there are many who think nothing of following us inside when we return even up to the very door of our suite and, if they are able, beyond. Ah, Queen Victoria, poor woman. At least upon my return home I will be able to fade into the shadows of welcome obscurity. You, alas, will experience the adulation of the masses, including their noise and smells for as long as you sit upon the throne.

Thinking of our dear queen puts me in mind of how Mr. D. and several of his cronies reacted when they learned of her marriage to her cousin Prince Albert. After imbibing a shocking quantity of spirits they went into the streets late at night shouting and waking the neighborhood. While they were imbibing, Mr. Dickens set the tone for the evening by acting the broken hearted lover distraught at his lady love's marriage to another. And he a married man with children! "Oh, Victoria, my queen, how could you do such a thing to one who loves you so," he cried out. And the others took up the theme and tried to outdo one another. Then out in the streets it was cries of heartfelt love, heartbreaking betrayal and future lifelong despair they shouted at the tops of their voices to the embarrassment of many, not least of which was the wife of the most heartbroken of them all. And it was a foolish laugh and, an, "Oh, Kate," when he came home and saw the look on my face. Needless to say, in his condition it was I who undressed him and put him to bed then spent a sleepless night wondering what my neighbors would have to say in the morning. But now with the passage of many months since Her Majesty's union with her consort, the pain of embarrassment I felt at my husband's behavior has been replaced by amusement every time I think about it— to have been jealous of Queen Victoria, ridiculous! And if my husband, on occasion, did not let loose and run amuck, as it were, so fulminating are his creative juices, I fear he would burst. I am even able to look, if not kindly at least toler- antly at the turmoil he stirs up with the children now and then.

In half an hour the house is in a shambles with everything where it shouldn't be, the children's clothing and toys in a jumble, shrieks and the clatter of running feet pounding through every room Mr. Dickens' bellows of laughter the loudest of all.

Seventeenth February, Thursday, Carlton House.

I do not like this city!!! At its heart there is something that can only be defined as cruel. Now London has its desperate slums with back alleys peopled by cutthroats and poverty-ridden women who are forced to offer their bodies for sale. But what fortune-favoured Londoner would even consider exhibiting these sorts of tragic places to visitors to their city? Not so here in New York. Mr. Dickens and I were paraded through portions of Five Points, one of the most dreadful, broken down, rat infested, foul smelling enclaves on earth. Never have I viewed such a collection of malnourished, vacant eyed, filthy, consumptive appearing human beings (if one can call them that) in my life. I was horrified that such a tragic place should be viewed by New Yorkers as being worthy of exhibition to visitors to their city. Needless to say, we visited the Tombs Prison at Mr. Dickens' request. But I have no doubt we would have been escorted there anyhow. I can scarcely bring myself to recount even a portion of the horror that met our eyes in that place: windowless, vermin-filled underground cells packed with everything from drunks to those awaiting trial for murder; a cell scarcely twenty feet by twenty which at times, according to the policeman in charge, contained as many as twenty-six women. Faintness and an uneasy stomach caused me to be ushered out of the prison. But later, Mr. Dickens told me about a young boy, no more than ten or twelve years of age, emaciated and miserable looking who had been locked up for weeks. And what was his crime? No crime at all. He had witnessed his father killing his mother and was being held in this underground cell as a witness. Then when Mr. Dickens made some comment about this being hard treatment for a witness, the guide replied to him: "Well, I don't know. It ain't a very rowdy life and that's a fact." Yes, here in New York there exists a general atmosphere reflecting a lack of compassion or at least a lack of interest in the less fortunate. Be they slum dwellers, prisoners, inmates of asylums, charity hospital patients, even fatherless and motherless children confined to prison-like institutions that put one in mind of Oliver Twist but from the filth, dampness and crumbling walls surely a cut or two worse than that institution where poor Oliver pleaded for a second bowl of porridge.

With all the hundreds of thousands here in America

who have read my husband's book (surely most of the literate people here in this city), how do such dreadful conditions continue to exist? The changes underway in England since the publication of Oliver Twist are truly remarkable and the orphanages in Boston and in New England appear to be compassionate and reasonably comfortable places. Thus how can I not conclude from the treatment of orphans here that this city's heart is devoid of compassion and kindness? When you add that to the pleasure of displaying to visitors slums, the deplorable conditions of the prisons and all the rest, the word cruelty and no other comes to mind.

Nineteenth, February, Carlton House, Saturday 2 am

Sleep continues to elude me. So after tossing and turning for an hour—Mr. Dickens is so soundly asleep I doubt if a pistol discharged next to his ear would wake him—I decided to seek refuge from this insomnia, a product of all the tumult of the past evening, by unburdening myself in this journal.

It was the evening of the Dickens dinner held at the City Hall. The noise, confusion and constant press of people trying to have a word with Mr. Dickens was no worse than expected and I would have struggled through without excessive damage to my nerves had it not been for Mr. Washington Irving. Now he, although famed as Mr. Knickerbocher, in no way resembles your typical New Yorker. In fact you would be hard pressed to compare him even with the better class of New Yorkers who do not reflect those elements of cruelty, or perhaps it is indifference, I dealt with in my last entry. Mr. Irving is a lovely, dear man who would be held in the highest regard by the most refined element of English society. If there is any man here in America I could love, as a friend of course, it is Washington Irving. He is warm but not effusive; gentlemanly but not artificial and modest almost beyond belief. Poor Mr. Irving, who was to preside at the dinner, began to exhibit the most dreadful nervousness hours before it was scheduled to begin. For he dreaded the dire necessity of making a speech almost as much as the convicted felon dreads boarding the cart which will carry him to Tybourn. This nervousness was not without its effect on me; being so fond of the man I was particularly vulnerable. Then, finally, when he rose to speak, someone called out: "Admirable! Excellent!" which threw him off his balance, so that he forgot he had his speech with him and after several unsuccessful tries all he could say was, "I give you Charles Dickens, the literary guest of the nation," and then stumbled back to his seat. I truly believe I suffered as acutely as did that poor man and I actually grew faint and had to resort to my vial of salts and dabs of cold water on my forehead and throat. After that, the noise and excessive warmth of the place and all the comings and goings of people grew close to unbearable. How I managed to remain at Mr. Dickens' side for the rest of the evening I do not know. Not one wife in a hundred, feeling as I did, would have forced herself not to retire and to continue to experience such suffering.

Well, even if I am unable to enjoy the relief sleep will provide, at least I am safely ensconced in our suite and the city outside the windows is quiet except for the occasional rumble of a late night cart made mournful by the clop clop of the poor beast dragging it along the cobblestone street. I must say my heart still goes out to poor Mr. Irving for the anxiety and embarrassment he suffered. I can't help but wonder if he also lies awake in his charming neat-as-a-pin house uptown. If so, I send through the ether my affection in the hopes it may soothe him and enable him to sink into much needed slumber. Well, that was a rather poetic sentence I just penned, unquestionably some atoms of Mr. Dickens have rubbed off—who knows what ten or fifteen more years of close proximity to the man will produce in his otherwise untalented wife. But truthfully, there can be no doubt that being constantly with Mr. Dickens has had its impact on me, and I am afraid it has not all been good.

One thing people could always say about young Kate Hogarth was that she was a practical, down to earth person, not given to the superstitious nonsense so often evidenced by other females her age. And it was that quality of no nonsense steadiness that my dear father most admired. I regret to say that my poor mother did not enjoy like admiration and for good reason. So little did superstition affect me, I would laugh when a black cat crossed my path; deliberately walk under a ladder and made it a point of spilling a bit of salt at the breakfast table with never a pinch thrown over my left shoulder. But these years spent with Mr. D. have eroded my freedom from superstition, and now the hoot of an owl or the midnight howling of a dog can set me off. For, although he attempts to hide it from the public eye, of all men, my husband is among the most superstitious and a close examination of his works will reveal that which he attempts to conceal during his normal intercourse with members of the public. On occasion, his vulnerability to superstition can result in what can only be described as household turmoil, most recently coming close to the cancellation of this trip to America.

Although carefully instructed not to make use of a slingshot his father made for him using strips from an old rubber sheet, Charlie apparently suffered a lapse of memory and shot a small stone, accurately of course, into the center of the hall mirror causing a pit in the upper portion of the mirror with inch-long cracks radiating from it like spokes on a wheel. Although the damage surely reduced the value of the mirror, it was not sufficient to cause its removal, and with a bit of bunting hung from the top it was scarcely noticeable. But when he was informed of the accident, Mr. Dickens' face turned the color of slaked lime, his eyes shifted rapidly from side to side, he clasped and unclasped his hands and a sheen of perspiration formed on his forehead. "Seven years bad luck, Kate," he managed to whisper. "And we in the process of preparing for a crossing of the Atlantic." His legs started to buckle and he sat down hard on a little bench facing the mirror and held his head in his hands. "What are we do Kate?" he murmured. "I know of cases where a mirror was broke and a death followed within half a year. And it is seven years of who knows what sort of adversities we face." With a groan he sprang up and rushed to the children's room where I found him with the baby on his lap and both of his arms desperately trying to encircle the other three.

Need I say that the Dickens' household was turned upside down for the next two days. Mr. D. did not write a line although he kept walking in and out of his study yet avoided his writing stand as if it contained some sort of deadly infernal device. I do not know what would have happened to my sanity had Daniel Maclise not happened by to whom Mr. Dickens immediately poured out his soul. That good man maintained a serious expression all through my lord and master's tragic account, nodding from time to time and making understanding sounds deep in his chest. Finally, he asked to see the unfortunate mirror and we trooped down the hallway as if on our way to a wake. Once there Daniel cocked his head, muttered, "Ah ha," then brought his face up close til his nose almost touched the glass, and then he stepped back and cleared his throat. "You have nothing to worry about, Charles," he said in a voice that rang with certainty. "The mirror has suffered a small damage, but by no stretch of the imagination can it be counted as broken. With that bit of bunting there, the pit is scarcely visible. The mirror still hangs in its accustomed place and continues to provide unimpaired reflections and unless young Charlie is determined on its destruction it will outlast you and Mrs. Dickens and may very well be used by your female grandchildren, if not great grandchildren to primp before leaving the house."

Mr. Dickens clapped his friend on the shoulder, then grabbing him by the hands, danced him around in a circle while all the children laughed, the baby included. And so ended this episode which if not for Daniel Maclise, might have caused my husband to actually cancel this trip. Such an action would have almost broken his heart, although, to be sure, any tears that I might have shed might just as well have come from the eyes of a crocodile.

Feeling my eyelids growing heavy, I will lay aside my pen, but not without first caressing my dear journal for the comfort it continues to give me. Would that I was able to properly thank Daniel Maclise whose gift it was. No better friend has ever lived.

Twenty-first, February, Carlton House, Monday.

Til now I have assiduously avoided mentioning Mr. Dickens' recently acquired bosom companion, Cornelius Felton. They met at Harvard College where Mr. Felton is professor of Greek literature and, it would appear, that this meeting was love at first sight. He certainly is a harmless fellow, good humoured, always smiling, his gold rimmed spectacles glittering and at times turning his eyes into tiny twin suns. From the moment the two men met, Mr. Felton attached himself to my husband and, in all fairness, I must admit he has been quite useful in helping us with the details of our journey; smoothing the way as it were. But enough is enough. It is time the man returned to Cambridge to resume his tutorial duties. Here in New York he has become so attached to Charles it is almost as if they had somehow been joined together as Siamese twins: Pickwick, Barnaby, and the rest being the membranes which cause this attachment. They parade up and down Broadway stopping at every oyster house and consuming such great quantities it is a wonder they haven't grown shells by now. Hours when Mr. Dickens has no engagement, when he and I could spend some domestic time together, have been usurped by Professor Felton. I shall undertake a campaign of gradually increasing coldness til I have pried them apart and sent Mr. Cornelius Felton on his way.

In the first year or two of my marriage there was no one more eager for Mr. Dickens' success than I. Even the briefest mention of his name in the local press sent a flood of delight coursing through me. I urged him to accept every invitation to appear before the public, even when the expected audience was unlikely to exceed two dozen. And those times, when things did not look too promising, I masked a sinking sensation and did all in my power to encourage and reassure him for he was acutely sensitive to these reverses and would sink into a deep funk where there was much sighing, and writing became so bitter a chore he was scarcely able to complete more than two or three pages a day. But now the worldwide fame my husband enjoys, with every prospect of it growing even greater, has become a heavy burden. Daily I feel the threads of our relationship weakened as ever growing masses clamour for him. In ways he belongs to the world and I must accept that. But I do not need to accept the likes of Mr. Felton who want him for themselves alone. Trust me, I shall send this professor packing. Would that I had the skill and the opportunity to serve Mr. John Forster in like matter.

Needless to say Mr. Dickens at this very moment is engaged in writing an excessively long letter to my chief rival. All the letters he sent to me while we were courting, taken together, do not exceed in total wordage two or maybe three of his letters to Forster. Well, at least I have my journal to turn to and that is a comfort.

I am homesick. I remember when I was eight or nine being sent to spend a month with my mother's favorite cousin. I called her Aunt Clara and she was as kind to me as any aunt could be. And having no children of her own, she was always giving me little gifts, many of her own manufacture. I was petted and loved and shown every sort of consideration during that month. Yet I was miserable. Not a day passed when I did not ache with longing to return home. Now, although I am a grown woman with much experience of the world, I ache as I did when I was only a girl. But now I not only yearn for my home, but have the added pain of longing for my precious children whose condition I cannot know. Yet I do know that in their little hearts day and night there is an emptiness which can only be filled by a mother's love. Oh, my poor babies, how I miss you. Yet months must pass before I again am able to press you to my bosom. If only I had refused to accompany Mr. Dickens. If only—

Feminine delicacy should inhibit my mentioning this, but since I alone will ever peruse these pages why should I pretend a delicacy I do not experience at the moment? For the past three days Mr. Dickens has not exhibited any manifestation of his amorous nature. This is unusual except for those times when he is ill. When he went through that terrible operation for his fistula it was a month before his true nature was restored, poor man. But now I attribute what some women might call relief, but not I, certainly not, never, I attribute it to his puerile involvement with that Felton person. You have never seen two grown men act more ridiculous. Even as a young girl when I was in the company of one or another dear friend, I exercised a great deal more restraint on my behavior than do those two and my friends did likewise. Having long since mastered the art of the cold shoulder—several wives of the titled personages who have entertained us since Mr. Dickens reached his present height were masterful teachers of that special art— Mr. Felton, I promise, will get more than a taste of it in the coming days. I give him no more than a week and in all likelihood only half of that before he is on his way. Thank goodness the wide Atlantic separates the Dickens' household from that annoying man. He wouldn't last a month at either Oxford or Cambridge. But what can you expect from Harvard College, located as it is in a land whose history goes back a scant two hundred years. A land, thus far except for Mr. Irving and perhaps two or three others, that has not produced any men of even moderate genius. Professor of Greek Literature, indeed. Would that I had the courage to say something directly to Mr. Dickens, who continues writing that interminable letter to John Forster. But I am a coward when it comes to confronting my husband. At least most of the time. There have been exceptions, but these invariably concerned one or another of my darling babies all of whom he adores but, at times fails to use good sense and/or decorum when dealing with them. There have been times when, in less than five minutes, he has plunged the household into turmoil; shouting and waking the babies; dancing around madly with whatever child happened to be closest; throwing a ball in the parlour, putting all my bric-a-brac in jeopardy; playing galloping horsey with two at times three riding his back with half the furniture in the house going into disarray; bringing home live or recently alive specimens gathered on one of his furious walks for the amusement of the children causing them to smell horribly and exposing them to who knows what sort of contagion. During these sorts of episodes with the children, I employ frowns, throats clearings, stern looks and finally, if all else fails, admonition which is usually: "Now, Mr. Dickens, what sort of an example are you setting for the children." Invariably that causes him to give me a sheepish look followed by his slinking away and taking up his pen for the next four or five hours. There are some, my sister Georgiana being principal amongst them, who feel that Mr. Dickens' antics with the children are not only harmless but helpful in their development. Is bringing home armfuls of presents almost every day helpful? How will they ever learn the value of money of which, unfortunately, we do not have a limitless supply? And if the children engage in roughhouse when invited to the homes of some of the best families, what sort of impression will they make? Even with Mr. Dickens' towering fame, poorly controlled children, though carrying the family name Dickens, will be shunned except by those less desirable households where children behave in a like fashion. In this world, except for the most fortunate few to whom the rules laid down by society no longer apply, Mr. Dickens being one of this number, self control and mannerliness are the stepping stones to a respectable life and general approbation. Georgiana, Mr. Dickens' most ardent defender, herself has a bountiful supply of self control and as for her manners, they are impeccable. Why then should she wish for less from her nieces and nephews?

Just the sheer act of writing the above paragraph has caused me to reevaluate my ways in regard to the children. Some of Mr. Dickens' behavior with them may very well generate unfortunate results. Yet some of his antics, like letting them ride on him like a horse, singing loud and dancing in a circle and similar actions, really are harmless and give so much pleasure to him and to them. Thus when I am being critical it is only just to separate out harmless activities, that I may find irritating, from those that really have a harmful potential and only interfere when he is engaged in the latter. Easier said than done, especially during those several days of the month when I am most vulnerable.

First of March, Wednesday, Carlton House (still)

Oh, will we ever leave this wretched city!!! We were supposed to depart for Philadelphia two days ago, but I have been laid low with such a severe sore throat the doctor forbade me taking a single step out of my bed. Mr. Dickens also came down with a sore throat which caused him to cancel a number of engagements. But he is sturdier than I and bounced back after several days. Dare I admit I was jealous of his rapid recovery and was consumed with self pity as I continued to lie abed with him out flitting from place to place. But now without Mr. Felton's ceaseless companionship. Harvard called, thank goodness, and the professor with his gold rimmed spectacles answered.

I, for one, have had enough of New York to last a lifetime. Noisy, rude, foul smelling, congested, madly in love with itself pretty well describes the place. How a sensitive, kind man like Washington Irving can stand to be in and out of it so often I do not understand. During this illness he visited me several times and each time brought with him a soothing comfort that was deeply welcome. Now we are scheduled to leave for Philadelphia on Sunday and I wish it were sooner. And there is a small yet vocal coterie of New Yorkers who will welcome our departure. For Mr. Dickens persists in going about complaining to anyone who will listen how unfair the copyright laws are in this country and the many thousands of dollars it has cost him and will continue to cost. No one likes criticism, no matter how well intentioned. For right under a layer of criticism are the words: I don't like you. And there is nothing Americans, especially New Yorkers, are more hungry for than being liked. How different it is in England. Not a day passes, when Parliament is in session, without unfriendly questions being asked of the government which appear the following day in the newspapers. That the Englishman's skin is thicker than the American's is beyond doubt. I am surprised my husband has not been challenged to a duel because of his outspokenness, but so far so good. I can scarcely stand waiting for Sunday which is scheduled for our departure. Speaking of duels, I will reread Pickwick Papers and let that comical duel that was scheduled to be fought tickle my funny bone again.

Thursday, Eighth March, 1842, United States Hotel, Philadelphia.

The relief I experienced upon arriving at this City of Brotherly Love, after a difficult five hour mixed train and boat trip, was short lived. For the manager of this hotel not only billed us for the days we had rooms reserved but were unable to use due to my illness which perhaps is fair, but also billed us for food we were scheduled to eat, table d'hote. Now that was unfair and caused both Mr. Dickens and me to protest vociferously, but to no avail. Although our reception upon arriving in the city was on a par to previous receptions, the manager was unimpressed and, as they say, stuck to his guns.

As unpleasant as the train trips in New England had been, the two trains we were forced to board coming here made the earlier ones appear positively luxurious. On these trains they had what is called a gentlemen's car, to which men repair when they have the need to smoke. The car I occupied was directly behind that one and there was such a hurricane of spitting and the discharge of tobacco juice out its windows the air appeared to be choked with a brownish colored snow. Need I say how disgusting all of this is. With a majority of Americans being originally sprung from the British Isles where spitting and tobacco chewing is rarely observed, how they developed this stomach turning mode of behavior I fail to understand. Brass receptacles called spittoons abound. They are scattered about in every restaurant. Each hotel room sports at least one spittoon. And a spittoon is to be seen every ten feet in every public building. And this includes courtrooms where serious trials are underway with everyone from judge on down regularly spitting.

Each city in this land appears to have its own unique personality. The word which best describes Philadelphia is sedate. Even in the brief time we have been here one can sense the Quaker influence and not a few people who have come calling used Thee and Thou and other Bibleisms as part of their normal speech. There is a certain charm in this and I have prolonged the greeting of men and women dressed in the old-fashioned manner of that sect an extra minute or two just to hear them talk. What little I know of this well kept and subdued city comes from what I have read about. Benjamin Franklin, formerly one of its chiefest citizens and unquestionably America's leading scientific mind. I can think of no one I would rather have met than Mr. Franklin, but alas, I have arrived fifty years too late.

Yet I have met one resident of this city who not only impressed me by his physical presence: a worn looking man, old before his time with piercing brown eyes and a soft voice echoing the deep south, but a voice that commanded attention, whose several works I read not only impressed me but overwhelmed with their force and mystery. I am referring to the author and poet Edgar Allen Poe. Despair was etched into his face. His hands trembled and without question he had been at the rum bottle. Yet still there was an intensity about him, and an energy, if you will, that I have seen in only one other man: Mr. Dickens when he is in his full literary stride. Moments after Poe was ushered into our suite, my husband embraced him. And I was startled to see tears in Charles' eyes. Yet now that I think about it why should there not be tears for this disintegrating man whose every printed word Mr. Dickens has consumed, and who he has acknowledged to have been an important influence in the composition of Barnaby Rudge.

Poe said little, but it was obvious he had been affected

by Mr. Dickens' reception—he kept holding the man's hand for several minutes after they were seated on the sofa.

Before Poe left a scant half an hour later, Mr. Dickens offered to do whatever was necessary to secure an English publisher for him. Although popular in America and to an extent in France, for some reason Poe had been mostly neglected in England except for the relatively small coterie of which my husband is a leading member.

After the poor man was gone, Mr. Dickens sighed as only he can sigh and bemoaned the near certainty that this remarkedly talented man was not long for this world. One thing I will say for Mr. Dickens, regardless of his mood, even when he is in a deep brown study, he displays not so much as a trace of jealousy toward other writers. In fact, he revels in their success and has been instrumental in helping various ones achieve it. From my not inconsiderable contact with other authors, several of whom having worldwide recognition, (I shall mention no names) jealousy toward their fellow labourers in the writers' vineyard is commonplace and nothing seems to please them more than the failure of a book penned by another to catch on. And talk about harsh critics! Give three out of four of them a chance and they will attack a book with hammer and chisel til it is scattered about like confetti. Yet, although Mr. Dickens has a highly developed critical sense, I have never heard him

attack the work of another. He may put a book or a manu-
script down after reading several pages and not pick it up
again, he may set aside a book with a sigh after reading it
halfway through, but at least, to my ears, never any criticism.

Mr. Dickens and I talked for awhile this afternoon. He
was subdued and allowed that he had been thinking about
the children and missing them as did I. Then we shared
impressions of the city: Mr. Dickens did not like the orderliness of the streets of Philadelphia, declaring its brick pave-
ments were distractingly regular and he longed for a
crooked street. In contrast, it is this very orderliness, creating a feeling of tidiness that attracts me. It's amazing in how
many things he and I disagree, yet we continue to love each
other as much as we did the day of our marriage.

How I remember that day: I broke out, my face was
swollen; I lost my balance and had to hold tightly to my
father's arm to keep from sprawling and by the time the fes-
tivities were over I had developed a shocking cold. While
Mr. Dickens was his ebullient self, storing impressions in
his capacious brain for later literary use. And through it all
I was numb. Although deep inside a small plaintive voice
cried: "Will this day never end."

March 11, Friday, Washington D.C. ,
Fuller's Hotel

We arrived in this city Wednesday evening after yet another abysmal train trip, this through Maryland where out the window we could see black slaves labouring in the fields—my first sight of human slavery. And although I certainly knew a good deal about it, actually seeing men and women in bondage was deeply unsettling. Maryland being one of the border states, how much worse must this peculiar institution be further south. Needless to say my husband was just as affected as I and he pulled a long face, bit his lower lip and was only minimally responsive when passengers on the train came up to greet him.

Now Washington D.C. is a city whose climate must vie for top honours in being the worst in the world. A scant two days here and we have roasted and practically frozen by turns and the mosquitoes and roaches and bedbugs, oh my. But far more distressing than the climate is the sight of tens and hundreds of slaves scurrying through the streets or engaged in menial tasks and this being the capital of the nation. If it contained the beauty of ancient Athens, it would still appear ugly to me with its cruel stain of slavery.

Perhaps because of Mr. Dickens and my so detesting this institution manifestations of which we saw all around us—

the very waiters, maids and porters in our hotel were slaves —we grew closer and comforted one another as we settled into our rooms. How much Mr. Dickens would have liked to rail against what he saw as would I, but not only would it have fallen on deaf ears, slaves being valuable property, but knowing the volatile nature of so many Americans it could have actually been dangerous.

I suppose we English have no right to be so righteous regarding American slavery. For surely half the slaves snatched from their native Africa and brought here were carried in ships flying the British flag and many a great English fortune is stained with this African blood. But at least it has been long years since we engaged in the slave trade. Yet here, in this part of the country, slavery continues to flourish as it has for the past 300 years. I shall tip those who serve us as lavishly as possible. Perhaps in this wise I may be able to help a mother purchase a child of her bosom from the one who owns him.

The only comfort I get staring out the window at the worn black faces that pass is Mr. Dickens' constantly repeated refrain: "It can't last. The people will not allow it."

Fifteenth March, Tuesday, Washington D.C., Fuller's Hotel.

I never thought I would regret, even for a single

moment, the departure of that Professor of Greek literature, but Mr. Dickens is mooning about so much wishing Felton was still with us I can see in his face that, in fact, a deep affection developed between the two men and that my jealousy, for that was what it was, puts me to shame. A wife's first responsibility is to her husband, not to herself. And when that husband is, as he has been referred to by some of England's most prominent citizens, a national treasure, a wife's responsibility is even greater. At this very moment my dear husband is writing to Felton and from the set of his features I can see how deeply he misses the man.

The Secretary of State, second in succession to the presidency after the vice-president, the renowned Mr. Daniel Webster called on us at the hotel. Of all the famous and would be famous who have called on us since our arrival in America, and they must total in the hundreds, Mr. Webster was the most artificial, the most posturing, the most self involved of the lot. Mr. Dickens declared he was the only unreal man he has met on our journey. I am less kind. There have been others. But Mr. Webster takes the cake as the expression goes. Every gesture declared how great was the burden this poor man carried. He rubbed his forehead, sighed, sat down heavily gripping the armrests of the chair shaking his ponderous head. And when he spoke, it was as if he were addressing the Senate of which he had so long been a member. He is the reigning prince of unlikable men in my view, and, I understand he is widely detested. Yet, somehow, he retains his grip on considerable power. We accepted an invitation to a levee at his house, how could we have done otherwise, but refused an invitation to dinner. Imagine sitting through an entire meal with such a pompous boor. Indigestion would be the least we could expect. Now, Henry Clay, who called on us shortly after our arrival in this capital, is another thing altogether.

Mr. Clay is the warmest, kindest, most self effacing (despite his considerable political power) man you could ever wish to meet. Second only to Washington Irving in my estimation, and a close second, this leader of the Senate truly brightened our day and continues to do so as he pops in and out. Following his advice, we are altering our plans and eliminating a visit to Charleston, South Carolina. Aware of my lack of robustness when it comes to travel, needless to say my face is still moderately swollen, he spoke of the poor condition of the roads, the deplorable state of the rail-road, the scarcity of decent accommodation along the way, and to hear a man of his exalted position freely revealing such inadequacies in a large section of his nation only con-firmed our opinion of Mr. Clay: A prince amongst men.

Mr. Dickens was invited to visit both houses of the Legislature. I suppose I could have tagged along but to tell the truth I had a belly full, as they say, of the adulation showered upon him. Crowds everywhere he went, etc, etc, and I just wasn't up to witnessing the honorable members of both houses rising to greet him (as proved to be the case) so I went shopping accompanied by dear Mr. Putnam and not a single soul recognized me. Would that I could honestly say that that was a complete relief but, to my shame, as we elbowed our way through the multitudes in the heart of the city without a single man or woman more than glancing at me with no sign of recognition, I experienced a pang or two of jealousy. Without Kate Hogarth things would be quite different with Mr. Charles Dickens I warrant. So much for my feminine pettiness. But when strong feelings rise up in one's bosom it is not easy to suppress them.

Although several days have passed since a certain event took place, I have deliberately refrained from recording it here to allow myself a little time to digest all the details of said event:

The morning after our arrival, accompanied by Mr. Daniel Webster, Mr. Dickens and I enjoyed a private audience with the president of the United States, Mr. John Tyler. Now it is my understanding that Mr. Tyler was originally elected vice president, a position viewed as relatively unimportant, one that has practically no responsibilities attached to it other than presiding over the Senate. But with the sudden death of the elected president after a scant month in office, Tyler was elevated. Even before we arrived in this capital city we heard from scores of people disparaging remarks about this second choice president as they referred to him.

Upon entering the White House, where President Tyler resides, we encountered dozens of gentlemen and some ladies strolling about, making free with the furniture on which some rested their boots while examining pictures on the wall. But what shocked me and stunned Mr. Dickens was the freedom with which the men present engaged in spitting. Some whose aim was unerring deposited the globules in the receptacles provided. Others less accurate left behind tokens of their visit to the building housing the chief executive of the land on the carpets, on the walls and here and there on the feet of an odd piece of furniture. Not one gentleman had removed his hat and the ladies were all chatter, chatter, chatter. Upstairs where a more favoured group awaited an audience with the president himself, there was perhaps a little more decorum. At least those who spit were more careful and whatever chatter took place was partially subdued. We were quickly ushered into the private chambers of President Tyler by a black servant in plain clothes and carpet slippers and there, next to a hot stove sending off waves of stifling heat, sat the president, all alone, and at his feet was a spit box of which he made use now and then as the need arose. The appearance of the man was ghastly. Exhaustion was etched into his features and he could easily have been taken for a man well into his seventh decade. As near as I can remember, the exchange between the two men was: President Tyler, "Is this Mr. Dickens?" Mr. Dickens, "Sir, it is." President Tyler, "I am astonished to see a man so young, Sir." For a moment I thought Mr. Dickens was going to return the compliment, but how could he have and not blushed with embarrassment. Then Mr. Dickens introduced me, but Mr. Tyler made no effort to rise or take my hand; merely nodded. Then he said in a tired voice, "I am happy to join with my fellow citizens, in warmly welcoming you to this country." With that, still seated, the president offered his hand which Mr. Dickens solemnly shook. And then he took a seat opposite the president while I took one to the side and for the next ten minutes the two men stared at each other without a word til finally Mr. Dickens said something about the president's time being fully occupied and that he had better go. To this the president nodded, spat, smiled a wan smile, then as we turned to go he sighed and spat again. I will give him credit for his accuracy in spitting, but then the spit box was close at hand and one could not help but wonder how it would have been had the receptacle been located a bit more distant.

In the days that have passed since this memorable visit, I cannot help comparing what I saw with receptions I have heard about at Buckingham Palace or even those that regularly take place at number 10 Downing Street. My God, spit boxes! Should our good queen ever visit this nation. . . I shudder to even think about it. Needless to say upon our return to our hotel, Mr. Dickens who had been as solemn as a judge through it all, as soon as our door was securely closed, started whooping, tearing off his waistcoat and vest, flailing his arms like a madman as he spun around the room making pretend spitting sounds to my exaggerated disgust and repeating almost at the top of his voice, "Spit boxes, spit boxes all on display at the White House, with President Tyler chief spitter of them all. This was a day to remember I'll tell the world. Spit boxes, spit boxes!"

Seventeenth March, Thursday, Richmond Virginia

The several hours' trip from Washington to this place has left me terribly upset. Passing farms and tobacco plantations on which ragged black slaves toiled from sunup to sundown and this includes children no more than five years of age, had a dreadfully depressing effect. Added to that was the bumping on indifferent roads and some peculiar tasting water I was unfortunate enough to drink.

I really do not know what I would have done if those letters from home hadn't arrived via the Caledonia three days ago. Seeing those poor black children out in the fields brought a rush of thoughts about my own darlings. Thank God they are well and the news of the baby bringing forth those teeth made me feel all warm and loose inside. I am so thankful they are with the Macreadys even though several of my intrusive acquaintances, after stating: "It's really none of my business but. . ." raised questions about leaving my children with people not related to Mr. Dickens or myself when both of us had fathers and mothers alive and well. And, "Wouldn't it have been better to leave the little dears with their very own grandparents?" Of course, I cut them off with smiles and: "Mr. Dickens thought it best," and the mention of his royalness's name had its desired effect but, in truth, the decision was essentially mine with Mr. D. concurring.

I suppose he would not have raised any objections to the children being placed with my family. Yet that would have been out of the question. My father, being heavily involved with his editorial work, my mother none too strong and quite overwhelmed with her household tasks (although many of them have been transferred to Georgiana) to say nothing of a lack of room in the house for four little ones. And had I even hinted at the possibility of placing our children with his parents, Mr. Dickens would have had one of his volcanic tantrums: "Have you taken leave of your mind, Kate!" would have been the mildest thing he would have said had I dared make such a suggestion. For despite the affection he has for his father and mother, my husband has no illusions about who they are. His poor mother lives in a constant state of turmoil. She gives the appearance of being busy about the house but just follow her for as little as half an hour. She misplaces everything. I have lost count of how many times she has declared her purse or her reticule missing and that they must have been stolen. But of course they turn up the next day. Food is left out in the sun to spoil while a shoe or a hat can be found in the window cooler. That the house has not burned down a dozen times must be counted as one of God's miracles. For candles are left dangerously close to curtains; firescreens fail to guard fireplaces as often as they do; and there is that pipe of hers she smokes up in the garret. As for John Dickens, my esteemed father-in-law: he mixes truth with fancy so that at any given moment you have no way of knowing if what he is saying is the truth, partially the truth, or a product of his overactive imagination. As to his habit of lifting a gold half crown or two every time he visits and before Christmas he'll hunt down whatever shillings are about also, it is the bane of my existence since more often than not it is my household money I need to keep close at hand for tradesmen that he appropriates. Well, if you entertain the Dane you must expect to pay the Danegeld. But how could I even consider barring my husband's father from the house? As far as placing my poor darlings with their paternal grandparents—over my dead body with Mr.. Dickens stretched out with pennies on his eyes lying beside me. I must write the Macreadys to let them know how grateful I am.

As I think about how I refrained from opening their letter when it was placed in my hands, I puff out my chest in pride consumed as I was to learn the news. And how the minutes crawled by like hours as I waited for Mr. Dickens so we could open the precious letter together. His heartfelt appreciation at my restraint was gratifying and I did feel so noble as I rosebudded my lips and made a "It was nothing" gesture.

I would be remiss if I did not record here that "sentiment," in his own hand, sent to me by John Quincy Adams, formerly president of this nation and now an esteemed member of Congress and a supporter of Mr. Dickens' campaign for an international copyright law. Mr. Adams is a dear man full of Eighteenth Century flavour and as courtly as one could wish. His sentiment:

"There is a greeting of the heart
Which words cannot reveal—
How, Lady, shall I then impart
The sentiment I feel?
How in one word combine the spell
Of joy and sorrow too
And mock the bosom's mingled swell
Of Welcome! and Adieu!"

Twenty-second March, Tuesday, Baltimore, Barnum's Hotel.

Not being one to dwell excessively on the ugly and cruel, unlike my husband who weaves these into his writing with the goal of helping to ameliorate them, I am still struggling to rid my thoughts of the scourge of slavery we have been exposed to these two weeks. Here in Baltimore, as was true in Washington, slavery does not expose its most ugly head as was the case in Virginia as we traveled that desolate road to Richmond. Thank goodness we listened to Mr. Clay's admonition and did not venture further south to Charleston. Had the horror that met our eyes grown any worse, as it must have had we traveled on, I fear my constitution could not have withstood it and I must have suffered a total collapse. One small thing sticks in my mind, like a splinter that somehow invaded my brain, is a sign posted on a decrepit bridge. It warned against fast driving, penalty—for whites $5.00; for slaves 15 stripes. Can you imagine! Fifteen stripes, enough to flay half the skin off one's back. This sign more than anything else I saw on that short journey into the deeper south declared the viciousness of this "peculiar institution" that these Southerners so vigorously defend. I have little doubt that my dear husband will have much to say about this abominable yet perfectly lawful institution in his future works much to the chagrin of its defenders. And I shall delight in every word he sets down upon paper.

It never ceases to amaze me the way he has disciplined himself to think deeply for hours at a time about aspects of human behavior he thoroughly detests, while most, I chiefest amongst that number, will turn away in horror at those many evidences of mankind's depravity. But Mr. Dickens, not for a single moment, will allow himself this sort of relief. Yet this focusing on the cruel and inhuman rarely sours his disposition or burdens him with depression. With him, moodiness and depression come from other sources. And interestingly, these almost never involved physical discomfort or even severe pain. Witness his recent surgery for that fistula. During the actual sewing up with silver thread he was heavily dosed with opium and other than grunts and groans muffled by his pressing his face into a pillow so as not to alarm the children, things proceeded quite well. But later when forced to respond to the calls of nature and when his digestion demanded the withdrawal of the opium and he lay on the sofa in what must have been acute distress, he comforted the children with hugs and kisses, told them amusing stories at which he himself was the first to laugh, not once exhibiting a single sign of depression. And his mood, if not buoyant, was at least no darker than any of the rest of us and often brighter. One evening when the nurse we employed had to attend to some bleeding and Charles' eyes were dull with fever and at times his body stiffened with what must have been jolts of pain and through it all he continued to comfort the children and at times even managed to chuckle, when we were finally alone, I asked him how he had managed it in his condition. "Well, my dear Kate," he said (I remember his exact words), "I converted the pain into colour. Red and orange mostly."

Friday, March 25, Harrisburg, Pennsylvania.

I am close to being undone. My very teeth have been loosened by the jolting, pitching and rolling of a contraption the natives here have given the name coach. But it is unlike any conveyance ever seen on British roads and is more deserving of the name: torture machine. Built to accommodate twelve poor souls inside and as many as four upon the roof, its jolting exceeds anything I have ever experienced or even imagined. That it was stuffy and foul smelling within goes without saying—Mr. D. took refuge on the roof where he had to contend with a pair of intoxicated gentlemen one of whom tumbled off shortly after boarding and returned to the grog shop from which he had emerged. Of course there was spitting inside the coach into two community spit boxes and this proved to be a pastime enjoyed not only by the male passengers, but by two elderly females whose cheeks were distended with snuff. My face swelled half again its normal size during that twenty-five mile torture from the town of York. And when I emerged, had I not had Mr. Dickens on one side and my good loyal Annie on the other, I believe I would have collapsed and died right there on the highway and would have been glad of the release.

Oh misery, thy name is Catherine Dickens. Sleep eludes me, thus my turning to this journal for comfort—bless Daniel Maclise for providing it. And crouched here next to this flickering candle with snores from our neighbors on both sides forming a medley with Mr. Dickens' rising and falling musical offerings, I am filled with dread, yes dread, at the prospect of tomorrow's journey aboard a canal boat that is to take us to Pittsburg. Annie fears being scalped by Indians as we travel west and was in tears. I on the other hand, miserable as I feel now with the prospect of even greater misery, would welcome it. As for Mr. Dickens, I am certain he will find some way to talk the savages out of it; so vain is he about his flowing chestnut locks which he gives as many strokes of the brush upon awakening as do I—possibly even more.

Sunday, March 17—on board canal boat.

Will I ever set eyes on my poor children again! And I thought those days crossing the Atlantic were the quintessence of misery. At least aboard that ship Mr. Dickens and I had a cabin to ourselves, albeit one that was small and stuffy. Here on this canal boat, inching westward with dejected mules on the towpath straining against ropes that keeps us in motion, not only do we lack the privacy of a cabin to ourselves, we are separated, he to the men's cabin I to the women's, with more than a score of other sufferers crowded into each cabin. We sleep, if you call it that, on shelves stacked one on top of the other without sufficient room to even turn over. And the stench and the closeness of these cabins defies description. I do not believe I have ever felt so thoroughly dreadful in my life as I do now.

Everything hurts. Bones I never knew I possessed ache. I can hold nothing on my stomach. My head feels as if at any moment it will explode. And my face, my poor face has grown huge and whatever looks I ever had are lost. I don't know how my husband can stand to look at me so ugly have I become.

Unlike our trip across the Atlantic where he also suffered, at least moderately, here on this beastly canal boat he actually appears to be enjoying himself. Up before dawn after a night filled with snores and a continuing course of spitting (a thin partition separates the women's cabin from his.) Then off the boat in a bound and for five or six miles he jogs alongside the mules waving at other canal boats and farmers working out in their fields. Now what kind of a woman am I, more specifically what kind of a wife am I to resent my husband's robust physical condition and his ebullience?

When he was a fellow sufferer, I found it a little easier to bear my distress. Now—I should be ashamed of myself, but I am not. He flaunts it, that's exactly what he does. And this is nothing new. Back home it is his wont to set off on ten mile walks with one friend or another and proceed at such a pace that the friend is soon blown and waits by the side of the road to be picked up by Charles on his way back. I wonder if some of this comes from his shortness of stature?

Some of his friends tower over him. Most are several inches taller. Thankfully, he is an inch or two taller than I when I slouch which I routinely do when we are together.

Well it would appear I do not feel kindly toward my world-famous husband this morning. With the rest of the day, the night and part of the next day still facing us aboard this miserable vessel, the bitter bile of resentment bubbles inside me at having been persuaded to accompany him on this trip when my place should be with my babies who, at this very moment, must be pining for their mother whom they will not set eyes on, if she lives, for another two months. Ah, self pity, what a sweet nectar thou art. And with this precious journal, I can indulge in it to my heart's content while showing a stalwart countenance to the rest of the world. I will smile at Mr. Dickens (I smiled), I will wave at Mr. Dickens (I waved), I will force my features into the most pleasant expression possible for his occasional glance as he bounces along next to the mules, his hair streaming behind him, not twenty yards away. Where oh where does he get his energy? Certainly not from his father who could sit at table or before the fireplace longer than any other man I've ever known. And after hours of sitting, off to bed for ten or twelve then slowly up rubbing his eyes and yawning like a coach driver who has been at it on the highway all night. As for his mother, poor soul, she has but one speed and that is somewhere between stock still and slow walk.

Well, the people aboard this vessel love Mr. Dickens and doubtless will be talking about their trip with him for years to come. And, obliging as ever, he has read portions of Oliver Twist, mainly Sykes' death, with so much emotion and such hideous facial expressions several of the women were forced to reach for their salts. If, like Robinson Crusoe, he was ever stranded on a desert island, no matter how well supplied with food and drink, he would soon perish for lack of an audience. Yes, that's it. he draws into himself a portion of the energy of others. In a word, people are fuel to him. Yet a fuel that can never be used up no matter how frantic he becomes at times.

Wednesday, thirtieth March—Pittsburgh.

No words are sufficient to express my relief at being quit of that dreadful canal boat with its poorly washed odouriferous passengers and its unwashed, positively reeking crew—and all that tobacco juice: quarts, gallons, hogsheads.

What can I say about Pittsburgh that is not unkind? Well, perhaps it is a bit less smoky than Birmingham. Is that a kind statement? And its broken down sections are less broken down than those of London. (It is not entirely displeasing to damn with faint praise.) Well, at least most of the inhabitants are reasonably well washed; would that their linen was likewise. But I will say that this moderate sized city has its fair share of peculiar individuals—the kind my dear husband relishes to include in his various works. Take the red headed brothers for instance. Is it possible to conceive of two youths, the elder no more than fifteen, with countenances so fierce that the first time I set eyes on them I recoiled and took tight hold of Mr. Dickens' arm and was thankful that the mayor of this city had assigned a burly policeman to accompany us. Mr. Dickens referred to them as "young dragons." And I can think of no description more apt. Several hours later, as I was shopping with dear Mr. Putnam, Mr. Dickens having been caught up in a swirl of his local admirers, what to my horror should I see in the reflection of a shop window, but those same two red heads, leering and exposing teeth more suited to the wolf than the human. They did not approach us, they said nothing, but wherever we went there they were. When we emerged from half an hour in some shop they were waiting. And they followed us to the very door of our hotel—I have no doubt we will again enjoy their company on the morrow. I shall ask Mr. Putnam to carry a stout walking stick. Better safe than sorry.

What is this fatal attraction I have for some of the most

peculiar of our species?

Having been struck down by a severe headache several hours ago—perhaps those two red headed dragons had something to do with its onset—Mr. Dickens suggested forming a magnetic chain to magnetize me out of my suffering. After some protest, I finally agreed and, gathering up half a dozen admiring hangers-on, a chain was formed and within minutes I was in hysterics. But then a wave of relief washed over me and I enjoyed a blessed hour of sleep and upon awakening the headache was gone and I found myself sufficiently restored to reach for my journal and bury myself in its welcoming pages.

I have made a noble effort to keep my thoughts away from what lies ahead of us when we depart this rather boring city. (Other than being idolized there is precious little to do or see here; being idolized may be sufficient for Charles Dickens but not for his wife.) But I withhold nothing from my precious journal. The prospect of boarding steamboats, which are to take us to St. Louis by way of Cincinnati and Louisville, positively terrifies me. You hear all the time of their boilers exploding; of terrible accidents with loss of life. Mr. Dickens tried to reassure me by telling me our stateroom is in the stern of the Messenger (that is the name of the first floating coffin) and that when boilers explode the force of it generally blew forward thus we were on the safest part of the vessel. "When boilers explode!" What manner of comfort was that? I stared for a full hour at one of those steamships this afternoon. Sparks, smoke and an infernal noise belched from the smokestacks. Of course the boat was entirely wooden and I shudder to think what a chance unnoticed spark could do if it landed in the right place. Just the sight of that vessel with all its exposed machinery and barge-like appearance and I could feel my face beginning to swell. Yet I must be brave. There is no turning back, alas. Perhaps the Author of All Beings knowing that I am the mother of four helpless children will cause His face to shine upon me and grant me a safe passage. I certainly hope so.

Saturday, second of April, aboard the steamship to Cincinnati.

I am pleased to say that our cabin (suite would be an excessive description) aboard this steamboat exceeds in comfort and, yes, in roominess the quarters to which we were condemned crossing the Atlantic. If not for a continuing fear of boiler explosion, despite Mr. Dickens' poo-pooing, I might actually enjoy this portion of our journey. For we are so located that we can sit outside on a secluded part of the deck and converse while gazing at the passing scenery without disturbance from any of our fellow passengers. But then there are mealtimes whose pleasures, if not usurped, are at least markedly lessened by some of the most persistent and boring individuals one is ever apt to encounter. And the assault at my ears by their droning, snuffling, voices! What I wouldn't give for a well washed, British conversationalist who did not suck up his nose between every other word.

Aboard the canal boat there was sufficient reason for the passengers to be indifferently washed. (I do not excuse the tobacco juice dribbles and stains.) But here on this steamboat there is an ample supply of hot water—even metal tubs that for a penny an obliging black man will fill for a cleansing soak. Not to be disloyal to my sex, if I cannot forgive at least I can tolerate those of the opposite sex who have not acquired an appreciation of the benefits of cleanliness (after all did not the great Samuel Johnson say something about having no great love for clean linen) but when I see women, whose clothing declares them to be not of the poorer class, trooping in to dinner with their hands and faces indifferently washed and their necks, my God, a farmer could think of nothing but tilling should he set eyes upon them. I cannot restrain feelings of disgust and must discipline my face not to reveal these feelings. On occasion, I have been present in the women's washup room early in the morning and have observed various members of my sex dab thimblefuls of water on their hands and faces as if this liquid contained a powerful caustic and any greater quantity would surely cause their skin to slough off. As for asking that accommodating black man to prepare a tub for them, even if it was the black man himself who provided the required penny, I doubt if so much as one of my shipboard sisters would have risked a quick immersion. One and all, if you venture closer than five feet to them, your nostrils will be regaled with a sour odour. With the gentlemen aboard this vessel, due to tobacco and their natural muskiness, ten feet of separation would be advisable; twelve feet even better.

Complain, complain, complain, how I love to complain in these pages and everywhere else exhibit the stoicism I am generally known for—with certain exceptions, of course, when the position of the moon is least favorable. I must admonish myself for this latest spate of complaining. For it has been a long, long time, certainly before fame struck him down, that Charles and I have had a chance to enjoy one another as we have the past two days. In ways it feels like it did when we were courting. Only now with the years having woven our lives together there is so much more to talk about; both happy and sad. And it was I who summoned the image of my sister Mary from both of our memories.

I don't know where it came from, but passing a dense forest of tall trees that came right down to the river so that their branches overhung and cast rippling shadows, I said, "Mary would have loved the quiet and deepness of those woods." Charles' eyes filled with tears as did mine.

"She was so young," he whispered. "So gentle and trusting and beautiful." Tears ran down his cheeks and he caressed the ring he took from her dead finger. "What sort of a God is there who would take such an innocent, delicate creature in the first blush of her womanhood?" He lowered his face into his hands and tears seeped through his fingers which I gently wiped away with my handkerchief!

Wondering if I really believed it, trying to comfort him, I said, "She is in a better, far better place, my dear." He groaned and shook his head.

"She wasn't given a chance, Kate," he murmured. "It isn't fair." And then with a bellow, his face crimson, his eyes like those of a wild man, he leapt to his feet and shook his fist at the sky. A shudder went through me. If ever there was a moment when the ship's boiler would explode it was now. But the vessel continued on its tranquil way and Charles, breathing heavily, sat down and after several minutes looked up and started talking about the children, wondering if they had colds and what each of them was doing at this moment. I, too, was wondering and was about to speculate when, checking his watch and making a quick calculation, he muttered, "It is twenty past three here, thus twenty past eight at home." Then clearing his throat, with a half smile, "I shall be very cross with the Macreadys if our four children are not safely tucked in bed—very cross indeed."

"As will I, Charles," I said laughing. "But if I know our Charlie, it lacks a good half hour before that one settles down. And I wouldn't bet a shilling that Mamey is safely tucked away either."

"Oh that Mamey," Charles chuckled. "What a little lady she is turning into." Then we sat for a time holding hands, each thinking our own thoughts Finally Charles said softly, "Would that our children could have known their Aunt Mary. They would have loved her and her them." I murmured my assent, then gently released my husband's hand and went into our cabin for a private cry. But it was not for my dead sister Mary. Only one day after our anniversary, which Mr. Dickens insisted was today and then offered as an excuse the time differential when I gently corrected him, and so much of his emotions and thinking still was intertwined with Mary, dead these many long years. Would that he felt as deeply about a living wife as he does about the ghost of his wife's sister.

Fourth, April, Monday, 1842, Cincinnati.

What a charming town, oh forgive me, city (those communities that deserve this appellation are jealous of it.) Not fifty years old yet it has the feel of one of England's lesser cities whose history stretches back half a thousand years. And to find this well-laid-out place, whose dust bins contain all the rubbish not its streets, was a welcome surprise after passing through so much wilderness with here and there a collection of broken down houses, one would not dare call a village, inhabited, for the most part, by roving packs of ragged children who have developed begging into an accomplished art. Upon arrival at this city, we were greeted by a fair-sized gathering of notables and literary lady types. Which gathering rapidly grew into a crowd exceeding a thousand by the time we disembarked having been added to by less notable types who inhabit wharfs and dockside warehouses. By the time we reached our hotel the crowd had swelled to over two thousand by the augmentation of hundreds of temperance types gathered here from all parts of the nation for a joyous temperance convention. And it was amazing how the absence of spiritous beverages did nothing to lessen the noise generated by this contingent. If anything, they were the loudest of all. Of course we were serenaded. We always are serenaded. In some places three and four times a day.

Mr. Dickens declared we were "not at home" to all callers til after the completion of the midday meal. But we were joined at table, much to Mr. Dickens' annoyance, by a carefully dressed elderly gentleman of the Jewish persuasion. And by his equally carefully dressed and slightly younger private secretary, also Jewish, who kept referring to him as Reb. Mr. Dickens' annoyance was partially mollified when the elderly gentleman announced that he had read all of his works. But this change in attitude was short lived when the old man went on to say that the author had proved himself to be no friend to the Jewish people by his characterization of the evil Jew Fagin.

His face growing a blotchy red, my husband defended by declaring that such men as Fagin were scattered by the score throughout much of London and that he himself entertained not a trace of prejudice, but that by the addition of such characters he improved the quality of his works and that the "Reb" had no reason to berate him for exercising his literary perogatives. "I am a Jew," said the old man, "and I was offended; that should be enough. . ."

I could see that Mr. Dickens was badly shaken. He began toying with his knife and fork and had stopped eating altogether. I was astonished at how deeply the old Jew's words had affected him. No matter what, Mr. Dickens never stops eating when at table.

"Except for that Fagin character, I have thoroughly enjoyed and also have profited in my understanding by reading your novels, Sir," the old man said in a soft voice, but one that held much authority. "You have a profound understanding of the human condition, Sir, and, except for a few works, Tristam Shandy comes to mind, your humour and your fondness for your characters stand at the pinnacle of literary perfection."

Mr. Dickens stopped toying with his utensils and made a stab at a tender looking bite of roast beef well soaked with gravy.

"When I say fondness for your characters, I do not exclude that pitiful herdsman of parentless boys," the old man continued. "Thus, I know, Sir, that in your heart you harbour no animosity to members of my race. But that such a character as Fagin, now known to the hundreds of thousands if not millions who have read and enjoyed Oliver Twist, should be portrayed in such a loathsome fashion not only is no credit to you, Sir, but is harmful to my co-religionists for the portrait you paint can only inflame those already prejudiced and to the multitudes who have no personal knowledge of Jews it may serve to implant the first seed of prejudice. Thus my admonition when I first sat down at the table."

"The book is between covers and hundreds of thousands of copies have been legitimately sold, an equal number pirated," said my husband spearing another bite of meat. "What would you suggest I do?"

"With Oliver Twist nothing. With Fagin, my people will be forced to struggle, if I am not mistaken and I believe I am not, for the next hundred years. Your works will last, Sir, mark my words. But in future books. . .literary seeds that await germination in your mind much can be done to demonstrate your friendship to the Jews and thus counteract, at least in part, the effect of Mr. Fagin."

After that the four of us ate in silence, the only sound: the click of silverware on dishes. Finally as the old gentleman and his secretary pushed away their plates preparatory to leaving, Mr. Dickens said, "I shall employ the maximum of vigilance on those seeds you spoke about, Sir. I was a young man when I wrote Twist. You may depend on this."

Later at a gala reception for us, Mr. Dickens was somewhat more subdued than is his normal wont. The impact of that elderly Jewish man had been considerable. As for me, embarrassment was the major component of my feelings. My knowledge of those of the Jewish race, or should I say religion, is limited. The few I have come in contact with were either in the rag and bone trade, proprietors of second hand clothing establishments, or in the pawn brokering business. None of them even remotely resembled Mr. Fagin. But unlike my husband, I have led a sheltered life and have never ventured into the darker corners of London, as has he on many occasions, and I do not plan to in the future. The one Jew, who in no way fits the rag and bone category with whom I have had limited personal and extensive literary experience, is Mr. Benjamin Disraeli whose novels I have devoured and who now appears to be a rising political figure about whom both praise and condemnation is increasingly heard. Without a doubt, that elderly gentleman and his reserved secretary who shared our table were of the class of Mr. Disraeli whose gentlemanly ways are above reproach. Thus I cannot help but wonder if that young parliamentarian and well known author has entertained a like reaction to the characterization of Fagin as did his elderly co-religionist. (I have heard somewhere that Mr. Disraeli now professes to be an ardent church of England man. But once a Jew always a Jew as they say.) If a rising politician and author of Mr. Dickens' caliber has taken offence to portions of Twist it is an embarrassment indeed. And one I shall urge Mr. Dickens to remedy in future works lest he put out of his mind his promise to our lunchtime table mates. Yet, as Mr. Dickens said, there are scores of Fagins to be found in London, thus one can hardly blame an author who creates his works from the stuff of life for including such a character in a novel he penned when hardly more than a youth who had had very little contact with society.

Ninth, April, Saturday, aboard steamship to St. Louis.

Can one detest a river? perhaps a mother unforunate enough to lose a child by drowning in the Thames would come to detest that river. Who is there who could blame her? Yet my dislike of this accursed Mississippi if not the equal to that of the bereaved mother, is at least close. Not a quarter hour passes without this steamboat being struck by logs singly or lashed together in rafts. The heavier strikes rattling my teeth, the lesser ones only my nerves. At any moment this vessel might come stuck on a sandbar, we have scraped over, with much grating and shuddering, several already. Dead cows float by, horses, mules—at any moment I expect to see a human body bobbing in the foam. From time to time we pass the wreck of a boat that declares: any aprehension we might experience is well justified. Annie, my maid, lies below deck hors de combat. The poor thing is terrified. Every time the boat strikes one of those log rafts she cries out, certain that the boiler is getting ready to explode. And there are moments when I wish it would and get it all over with. If I die, I die. If not, I am on my way back to England and my precious children. . . Of course I don't mean what I said about the ship's boiler exploding. If there are any unseen eyes peering over my shoulder, please disregard a distraught woman's moment of foolishness. I would cross out the words if I hadn't decided to let whatever I enter into this journal stand and be immune to correction.

We stayed briefly in Louisville, Kentucky, after leaving Cincinnati. I had my first sight of a slave market and a firm of slave brokers and this threw a pall over my short stay in that slave-ridden town. Sweating, hollow-eyed blacks are everywhere. You scarcely see a white engaged in a task requiring physical labour. Most of the ones we saw were lounging about. Need I mention the streams of tobacco juice being discharged. Several of the bigger and older loungers were veritable fountains of that noxious brown liquid. It is quite a feat to walk the streets of this city, even the better neighborhoods, without getting one's shoes splattered.

A L.L. (literary lady), done up like one of those dolls costing two or three pounds displayed in shop windows at Christmas time but rarely purchased, approached me as I walked the street with Annie, who at that moment was so thankful to be quit of the boat there were tears in her eyes. "Lady Catherine Dickens?" the woman said, curtsying and blocking my forward progress. "Wife of Sir Charles Dickens." With the help of Annie who took hold of my arm and hurried me away, the L. L. being cut off, was left standing with an expression that added years to her doll-like appearance.

"The rudeness of some people," my Annie muttered. "Imagine blocking your way with that ridiculous curtsy and showing such an ugly expression when you chose not to enter into conversation—the two of you never having been introduced."

Although I tried to placate Annie and use the word rude myself, there was something not unpleasant being addressed as lady Catherine. And this incident set me to thinking.

Two hours later

There happens to be a "sir" aboard this vessel, at least that's what that scruffily dressed individual with a mid-Atlantic accent claims to be and there is much bowing and scraping, as he comes and goes with his rather pointed nose up in the air. Mr. Dickens is particularly amused, declaring there is a good bit more of this side of the Atlantic in his speech than the other. "Perhaps President Tyler has taken to creating peers," he said as the individual in question paraded past our dining room table with all eyes upon him. We happening to be at the captain's table, he and his first mate laughed good naturedly, but those at adjoining tables had horrified expressions and would have doubtless said something uncomplimentary had my husband been a personage of lesser note. "The very idea of suggesting that our president would even dream of creating peers. . ." their looks declared. And for an hour after dinner there was some slight exhibitions of coldness as we strolled the decks. But then, four strikes against log rafts within a quarter of an hour, and the anguish they engendered, caused whatever coldness that existed to dissipate and once again we were favoured with unrelenting attention til we were forced to seek the refuge of our stateroom.

Have you ever considered letting it be known that you would not be adverse to being mentioned in the Queen's annual list of honours?" I asked carefully after we settled ourselves in our room and were enjoying a glass of sweet wine made, I understand, from blackberries that grow here in profusion. At that Mr. Dickens burst out laughing. "Sir whatever his name is, who struts the deck, seems to have had an effect on you, my dear Kate," he said patting my hand as if I were one of the children. "There are many things in this life I want and will labour hard to obtain," he went on, "but amongst those things, being mentioned in the Queen's honours list does not exist even to the point that if offered a knighthood or other honour, I would reject the offer out of hand with all due apologies. And from knowing me and reading my various works, you should know, beyond a doubt, how little stock I put in this royal perogative of raising gentlemen to titles of honour. Fie, Kate," he said, "to having the temerity to even suggest raising someone to a position where he is able to lord it over somebody else."

Not pleased by Mr. Dickens' mocking laughter and his tone of voice, the collisions with those rafts having had a disquieting effect on me, I said, "I detect in what you just said, Mr. Dickens, elements of displeasure towards our Queen. I thought from your behavior the night of her marriage. . . "

"Hold your tongue, Kate," he interrupted in a voice so harsh I suffered several moments of faintness and had to reach for my salts. "I will not hear another word about the Queen or about honours or about titles." He brought his fist down on the little writing table so hard the flask of blotting powder fell to the floor with powder spilling everywhere. I really don't know what I would have done had he not stalked out of our room, probably fainted dead away. But having my precious journal to turn to after he was gone was a blessing for which I can never be grateful enough to dear Daniel Maclise. One thing is certain; I will never!!! say another word about Her Majesty's honours list. But you never know when Mr. Dickens will take offence, do you?

After all an author as accomplished or, dare I say, even more so, whose literary production far exceeded that of Mr. D. (of course Mr. D. is still a comparatively young man) was not adverse to accepting a baronetcy which, alas, now is dissolved at the unfortunate death of his son. I refer, of course, to the author of the Waverly Novels and to so much more. Sir Walter being so much better born than Mr. D., his father was a knight and his was an ancient family, the sort of excessive sensitivity displayed by my husband was not part of his inheritance. Accepting that baronetcy was as natural to him as breathing. But with a half paid pensioner for a father, who was always in debt and who had known the inside of a debtor's prison to say nothing of his practically helpless mother, who is all the time wringing her hands, what could one expect of the son other than an excess of sensitivity and a skin so thin that if one stares hard enough the bones and the vessels become visible. (I give thanks to God that my husband's eyes will never peruse this entry. But it has afforded me considerable relief which will enable me to face him with equanimity when he returns from what will be probably a hundred circumnavigations of the ship's deck at something just short of a run.)

Thirteenth, April, Wednesday, St. Louis, the Planter's house.

If one wishes to experience a frontier town, St. Louis certainly fits the bill. Located at the very edge of the vast, sparsely inhabited prairie over which savage Indians still roam, I am informed, (half the people here in their manner of dress, lack of cleanliness, roughness of speech, hardness of eye and carrying of knife and pistol being just as savage as any Indian) this city has made an impression on me, and I suspect Mr. Dickens, unlike any other place we have visited thus far. Walking the creaking wooden sidewalks, I both shudder and tingle with excitement. The way these rough looking men swagger one expects at any moment pistols to be drawn and shooting begin to determine who will give way to the other when two confront one another on the sidewalk. And I am certain if it were as little as half a foot narrower, so that they could not brush by one another without stepping into the muddy street, pistols would be drawn and shots fired every few minutes. Foolish woman that I am, there is that within me that would not be adverse to witnessing such a confrontation—I would die before admitting this even to my closest friend!

I am temporarily recovered from that Mississippi boat trip (we soon return to Cincinnati by boat) and my health has never been better since departing England. Even my face is back to its normal size and an occasional glance into the mirror confirms I am still not an unattractive woman. Yesterday, just before he left for an overnight experience of the prairie, Mr. Dickens informed me that the wife of one of this city's leading citizens had declared that from my speech she would have never believed that I was anything other than American. Can you imagine that! Not yet two months in this nation and already I have acquired the accent. What my family and friends will say upon my return can only be imagined. I can almost hear my dear father exclaiming, "Kate! What has happened to you—what have they done to you over in America?" It is strange, one cannot really hear one's own speech. I would have never believed I had acquired that nasal way Americans use our language. And I must confess it tickles me more than a little.

Mr. Dickens looked wan when he returned from that overnight out in the prairie, "It is vast, Kate," he muttered. "But there is a sameness that is almost boring. Give me a night on the Salisbury plain any time. There one senses a mystery, a magic if you will." He sighed. "What a disappointment." Annie, who heard all this and who lives in terror of Indians that she fancies lurk just beyond the city's limit was considerably relieved. I think she despaired of Mr. Dickens' return and did some quiet weeping at those times

I didn't keep her employed.

I suspect this disappointment (the Lord only knows what he expected to see out in all that emptiness) caused Mr. Dickens to grow so testy that he carried it with him when we left our very comfortable room to again venture amongst the multitudes. A certain local judge, whose name I failed to catch, fell victim to this testiness when he attempted to engage my husband in a discussion regarding slavery, the judge being an ardent defender of the institution. As Boswell said of Johnson, Mr. Dickens tossed and gored the unfortunate man who was no match for one of the world's most skillful wordsmiths. I have seldom heard Mr. Dickens unleash such a tirade outside the confines of his home. The poor soul who had introduced the judge to him, looked as if he would have been grateful had the earth opened beneath his feet and swallowed him up.

Why, I asked myself, if the prairie proved such a disappointment does my husband continue to display such ill humour that it verges on outright rudeness? One gets over disappointments doesn't one, especially when one's ears are filled with accolades and the town's leading citizens vie with one another just to exchange a word or two with you. When this ill humour continued through dinner and I could see that Mr.. Dickens was struggling not to be short with the mayor, the local congressman and the commander of the state militia who had joined us at table, it struck me that it was not disappointment with the prairie that so deeply disturbed him. I remembered how he had reacted, about a year after our marriage, when Charlie was scarcely a month old and we were awakened by what we both thought were burglars in the house. Charles plucked at the bedsheets as if struggling: should he go below stairs to investigate or remain safe where he was. "Bolt the bedroom door," I had whispered to him, "the baby is with us and that's the important thing." Mr. Dickens' face had grown ashen and I could see he was thinking about my sister Mary in her room across the hall. It took him two or three minutes before he finally left the bedroom to investigate after arming himself with a stout walking stick—sounds were still coming from down below.

The serving girl had left the rear door unlatched and two stray dogs found their way in and had done a moderate amount of mischief. I heard yelps as my husband used the walking stick to good advantage. But when he came back to bed, for the first time in our marriage, his mood was foul and he was so short with me I was in tears and then he just turned his back to me and pretended to go to sleep. But from his breathing I knew he hadn't. And the next day he was testy—even with John Forster with whom he had formed a tight friendship. It was obvious that he had suffered a terrible fright and that was the cause of this testiness. So, remembering that distressing episode, I couldn't help but conclude that my husband's experience out on the prairie had been anything but boring. Knowing him, I was certain he would never admit to having been afraid. Even during the worst of the storms as we crossed the Atlantic he made light of the situation. Not that he wasn't worried. But his reaction was different from that of the other passengers, myself included, and you could see he took pleasure in playing the stout-hearted one. And, because he was able to assume this stout-hearted role, the foul humour he exhibited after the "burglary" and exhibited now upon his return from the prairie was not in evidence. He used the word "vast" describing the prairie. At night out in the garden when I look upwards at the vastness of the sky and the myriads of stars there are times when I experience a hollowness inside my body as if in the face of all this vastness I am really helpless—it will all be here after I am gone. Perhaps that was what my husband experienced in the prairie. With all of his accomplishments and his fame, in time he will be gone, but the prairie, like the sky, goes on—forever.

Make no mistake about it, Mr. Dickens is a strange man. I wonder, had I known how strange, in ways how unfathomable, would I have married him. We have had four children together and, unless I am mistaken, it will not be too

long before we have another; we have shared the same bed
surely two thousand nights and have faced one another at
table surely six thousand times, yet in so many ways Mr.
Dickens is still a stranger to me. Not so I to him. Kate is as
familiar and reliable and comfortable as an old pair of bedroom slippers. Good old Kate! Well, Mr. Dickens, you are
lucky to have me. The way the earth rests on the shoulders
of Atlas, that is the way it is with us. Only for me there is no
great turtle to stand on. Only endlessly shifting sands that
may one day engulf me. I can't help wondering, Mr. Charles
Dickens, how you will fare if I and my shoulders should one
day crumble.

Saturday, Sixteenth April, aboard the Messenger on the way back to Cincinnati from St. Louis.

I was horrified, simply horrified to have been present
when one of the passengers on this boat regaled Mr.
Dickens with an account of a duel that took place on an
island near St. Louis called Bloody Island. This passenger
had been a second at this duel, fought with pistols breast to
breast, with both parties falling dead at the same time. What
a thing to say in the presence of a lady!!! In my last entry, I
did say something about men who might fail to give way on
wooden sidewalks going at it with their pistols, but that was

only the product of a foolish woman's imagination, and certainly a thing I would never reveal to another soul. This account by that boorish passenger was of a tragedy that actually happened. And what a difference that makes. Which leads me to the many grim and tragic happenings my husband weaves into his novels. In a hundred places in his works I have either shuddered or dissolved into tears as I read what his fertile mind had put down on paper. But always I was, in a manner of speaking, insulated by an awareness that what I was reading flowed from his imagination. True enough, he has witnessed much, has explored dark and dreadful places. I've listened to hundreds of accounts of people he met on his many explorations and his imagination has been fueled by all of this. But the death of Sykes on the printed page is quite different from a gory account of a fatal duel from one on whose hands blood has also left a shameful stain. Yet there may be some as sensitive, or possibly more sensitive than I, who are as affected by Mr. Dickens' printed words as was I from that passenger's gleeful serving of gore.

Which brings me to something that has long troubled me. As kind and sympathetic as Mr. Dickens undoubtedly is, with all the good works he has initiated and the many he supports, there is still the quality of the man that can best be characterized as macabre. Not once during the journey, no matter how small the town or obscure the village, has he failed to visit the local cemetery. Of course, he routinely seeks out prisons, orphanages, hospitals and work houses, but these visits can be justified by his endless quests for grist for his literary mill. But visiting all those cemeteries? And those visits of his to decayed old abandoned churches, to deserted houses, to the town morgue and often to where dustmen dump their sweepings, are not all of these reflections of a morbid mind? If you add to this, his fascination with ghosts and spectres the word macabre must immediately come to mind.

Before I was so burdened with children, I would take long walks with Mr. Dickens and surely a score of times it was to a cemetery he would lead me when I complained of fatigue. It was as if every churchyard for miles around was catalogued in his mind even bramble grown remnants of churchyards with the church building tumbled down. And how he studied the tombstones, at times picking away moss that he might read the inscriptions on the very oldest. More often than not he would read these aloud in a mournful voice, yet there was something in his face that told me he was really enjoying it. And more often than not upon our return after sojourning in one of those cemeteries, his amourous nature was especially evident.

Four hours later:

A little before midnight I was interrupted in the midst of my entry in this journal and what an interruption it turned out to be.

First a crash as the boat plowed into what must have been an oversized raft of logs causing the vessel to shudder and creak and I could hear sounds of crockery breaking. Then Mr. Dickens bursting into the room, an anguished look on his face as he dove into the steamer trunk where we kept our most valuable possessions and brought out the miniature of our four precious children.

"Standing on the deck, Kate," he gasped, "I saw a bundle float by—" Perspiration had formed on his forehead and his hands shook. "My heart almost stopped. . . .I thought it was a child, Kate, a little child. But then I could see it was only some rags and sticks tied together, but I had this terrible premonition, Kate. . . ." His words were choked off and he hugged the miniature to his breast for several seconds. "A premonition that something had happened to our children." Tears sprang into my eyes and my body started to shake as if from the ague. Without realizing what I was doing I snatched the miniature from my husband and sank down to the floor cradling it in my arms with tears flowing freely.

"A fire," I managed to say, the horror of the thought causing my eyes to go out of focus. He sank down to the floor beside me and put his arms around my shoulders. He too was weeping. I could feel his tears on my bosom. We both needed a good weep. Yet after a few minutes I began to feel foolish. People are always having premonitions and ninety-nine times out of a hundred it turns out that nothing is wrong. And when you think how many miles separate us from England—four thousand at least—how could a premonition travel such a distance? And that is what I said to Charles, but he didn't seem to hear and kept on weeping. "Now, Charles," I said, "I know how much you miss the children because I know how much I miss them—I think about them constantly and every night before I go to sleep I ask God to watch over them. And here in my heart," I placed my hand on my bosom, "I know they are safe and well, all four of them. It was the shock of seeing what you thought was a child floating in the river that brought that upsetting notion into your mind. And just as the floating child turned out to be a bundle of cloth and sticks, so your premonition will turn out to be something harmless that floats by and that's the end of it."

Drying his eyes on his sleeve, Charles gently took the miniature from me and studied the poor little faces while I studied his face that still showed signs of anguish. "I wish this damnable trip was over," he said in a soft voice. "I'm growing sick of all the arrogance, all the disgusting habits and the air of smugness so many here exude. I've had enough of America. And that I have received so little in the way of remuneration, although half the population seems to have read my books, continues to stick in my craw."

His face began to clear, but then clouded again. "Several hours before Mary died I had this premonition that something terrible was about to happen," he murmured. He was at it again, but this time I was determined not to let it affect me. Even though where the children are concerned I usually am as fragile as a piece of Dresden china. "I could feel it in my body, in my bones, my throat, my head just as I felt it just before, when that bundle floated by, Kate. I wanted to rush home and check on things. But I didn't—I might have saved her. . . " The weeping started again, but I wasn't sure if this weep was for the children or for my dead sister. He kept it up for surely a quarter of an hour. He was like a little boy and, may I be forgiven, there was a coldness in my heart and I had to force myself not to move away from him. I knew what was coming next—what always came after an outburst of emotion. And I did not want the amourous intentions of a little boy focused in my direction. In fact, I felt so cruel, a portion of me wished he would conjure up the image of Mary and have her be the recipient of his ardour. I don't know what I would have done had he pursued his obvious intentions, but fortunately he must have sensed my feelings and after the passage of another quarter of an hour, he stumbled out of our cabin and I drew in a deep breath that was part gasp, part sigh.

Then I put the miniature away. The children were just fine. And I determined to count the days til we boarded the ship which was to take us back across the Atlantic and try to enjoy each day as it passed.

Tuesday Nineteenth April, 1842, Cincinnati.

I uttered a sigh of relief when we finally disembarked back here at this charming city. It was about one o'clock in the morning and as we made our way to our old hotel Annie, poor thing, measured herself on the pavement there being a broken place and for several minutes, til she was able to get herself together, I feared she had suffered a serious hurt and my heart beat wildly as I tried to give her a whiff of salts while Mr. Dickens massaged her hands and said soothing things to her. The strangeness of this incident lies in the fact that my loyal Annie is as sure footed as a mountain goat, while I am the one prone to stumble and knock myself about. And I will say, it is to Mr. Dickens' credit that with two or three exceptions, he has restrained from commenting at my daily stumbles and bruises knowing how much I detest his calling attention to them. He is of the opinion that, if only I would be more careful and concentrate fully on what I am doing, I could avoid all these unpleasant mishaps. But the truth of the matter is: I expend a great deal of energy attempting to be careful—barking my shins is no great pleasure to me—yet despite all my efforts, I continue to be a mass of bruises, and it is a wonder I haven't broken any bones (toes do not count.) There are people who are stumblers and people who are not. Mr. Dickens, I believe, could race up one of the snow covered Alps, skipping from rock to rock, and bounce down the other side without a scratch. I have been known to sprawl face down on the floor bloodying my nose while getting out of bed. I do believe Mr. Dickens' laudable restraint regarding my stumbles and shin knocks results from my having howled for half a day during our Atlantic crossing when I attempted to leave our cabin, lost my footing and raised a lump on my head as I fell and his first reaction was: "Why don't you try and be more careful, Kate." After that I wept through lunch, through dinner and would have kept it up even longer had I not been overcome by fatigue and seasickness and fallen asleep. When we were first married his usual response to my difficulty was teasing. Then it was poking fun at me in the presence of others. But after the children started to come whatever annoyance or irritation he felt was expressed in private, although I am certain he bewails this defect in his wife to John Forster, his confidante in all matters, alas.

Well, I seem to have covered what in truth is a petty matter pretty thoroughly. In ways I am a small minded person. But, if I am, it can't be helped. So there.

Having declared myself, what other small minded matters shall I inscribe on these pages of vellum which deserve better? Shall it be the constant and unnerving interest swarms of those of my sex display towards my husband? Or shall it be the parallel disinterest by those of my husband's sex which is focused in my direction. (Can disinterest be focused?)

One of the most unfair things in life is the early fading of women, most of whom have seen their best days by thirty, and the way men seem to increase in attractiveness, coming fully into their own, between the ages of thirty and forty, often lasting well into their fifties. Child bearing surely is one reason. But I know a number of spinsters who do not lag far behind their married sisters. Yet we women place so much greater value on appearance and youthfulness than do men. With my husband, one of his greatest burdens, so he has informed me, is his extraordinary youthfulness. People are constantly amazed that this young chap, scarcely past his boyhood, fresh-cheeked, of bounding step, youthful of voice, is the mighty Charles Dickens, the inimitable. And it pains me to say that there have been some unkind people who have remarked about the strangeness of Mr. Dickens marrying someone so much older than himself. One old dowager took me for his mother when I was all swollen up with Walter, but the actual pregnancy had not yet showed. I took to bed for two days after that with a sick headache.

It frightens me a little put this down on paper—as if by so doing I set in motion forces that might cause it to come true. But I find myself growing increasingly anxious regarding Mr. Dickens' continuing affection for me. The thought of another woman entering his life is chilling. Yet I know that hundreds, if not thousands, of women would set their caps for him if given the chance. And there are the brazen ones who would willingly fall at his feet. . . . I cannot bring myself to say any more. Poor comfort I've gained this time from this journal. But I shall put on a good face for Mr. Dickens. His mother, indeed! What a thing to say. I shudder to think about that dreadful dowager—and here it looks like I am pregnant again.

Saturday, twenty-third April, Lower Sandusky, Ohio—Log Inn

I am bruised and nearly broken from the coach trip from Columbus to this dreadful place. Mr. Dickens hired a coach for our exclusive use and everything possible was done for our comfort (a hamper of delicious food and drink was placed on board for our pleasure and the driver couldn't have been more considerate or courteous.) But, oh the road! If one dare call that rutted, mud-filled rock-strewn, twisting turning thing a road. I and the others were bumped and jostled hitting our heads on the roof, bruising arms, shoulders and hips against the sides, constantly bouncing up and down, even gyrating on occasion. The only relief, and it was a welcome relief, came when we stopped in the woods (glorious pristine woods they were) to dine and we drank to all our friends and our dear children. But then on the "thing" again and it took all I could do to keep the meal I had eaten down.

I regret to state that there are bugs here in this small bedroom Mr. Dickens and I occupy. Before picking up my journal, while Mr. D. was exploring this primitive place, I went over the bed carefully and dispatched half a dozen of the pesky creatures. But I fear there are others lying in wait for us deep in the recesses of this well worn bed which rests in a boxlike structure affixed to the unplaned split log floor. At this moment Mr. D. is asleep and thus far has given no sign of those unwelcome guests. But I fear that when I snuff the candle and stretch out beside him noxious visitors will start to arrive.

Upon Mr. Dickens' return from his exploration of the local flora and fauna, I expected him to flop into bed fully dressed, except for his boots, as is often his wont after an exhausting day. But no. He stood in the middle of the room stroking his chin as he studied the two doors on opposing sides of the cabin. Each door led out to a stand of brush through which one had to struggle, there being no regular pathway on either side. "Why in the world did they put two doors in this God-forsaken cabin, Kate?" he said, deep lines of puzzlement showing in his forehead. At that moment a gust of wind blew one door open and the inrush of air caused the other door to swing open also. Using extreme care, as if the doors were of porcelain rather than ill fitted slabs of wood, he closed both of them. Several minutes passed and the first door sprang open again followed, after a preliminary shudder, by the other. "The wind is from that direction, Kate," he pointed at the first door. He said this with a seriousness a chemist might employ upon discovering a new compound. "Do you think the two doors have something to do with the direction of the wind in this place?" he said, peering out one door then quickly out the other. I was sorely tempted to say: Two gusts is hardly enough to conclude that the wind only blows in one direction. But I restrained myself. Among things Mr. Dickens likes least is to be corrected. Although to be sure, he is not above correcting others, his dear wife in particular.

"Well Kate," he said after several minutes of serious contemplation, "we had best do something about these doors. In their open state they will provide too much temptation to a passing burglar when we are asleep." I knew he was concerned about a moderate quantity of gold coins we were carrying. "Two doors," he muttered. "Strange, strange, strange." With that he moved a rickety little writing table that barely stood erect on its spindly legs next to the first door. "There," he said rubbing his hands with satisfaction. As if in answer a mighty gust of wind threw the door open followed a moment later by its companion. Of course the rickety table went flying halfway across the room. "That writing table was not sufficient," he said and in a voice that held an accusatory edge, as if I were the one who suggested its use. "Ah," Mr. Dickens exclaimed taking hold of our heavy portmanteau and wedging it against the offending door. Then tapping his foot he waited for another gust. Five minutes passed; then ten with no gusts. Mr. Dickens stuck his head out of the other door as if searching for gusts. But then, just as he closed that door, there came a mighty gust shuddering the cabin. The portmanteau door held quite nicely, but the other door, for some reason, sprang open. Mr. Dickens was incensed. He had gone beet red and I am certain, had I not been present, would have administered a kick at that willful door. Mr. Dickens, it would appear has this tendency to imbue inanimate objects with wills, prejudices, even with romantic inclinations. "So you want one too," he addressed the door. "Well, you will have to settle for a case and a small hamper." Saying this, he carried them over and secured the door, wedging the top of the hamper under the knob. "Now we shall see," with an expansive gesture he addressed the world. In reply came a gust, less mighty than the one before, yet of considerable force. Both doors held. "I shall speak to the innkeeper about these doors in the morning," he declared kicking off his boots and climbing into bed. "That sort of arrangement can only lead to disaster, don't you agree, Kate?" I nodded. I would have agreed had he insisted the moon was made of green cheese. Then he said, "Suppose the next traveler does not have a portmanteau of sufficient size. Something like that could lead to a suit at law, don't you agree, Kate?" I nodded. Anything could lead to a law suit. I smiled remembering poor Mr. Pickwick with his "chops and tomata sauce." Then I smiled at Mr. Dickens, but he was already asleep, a satisfied expression showing on his face.

I must confess that I secretly hoped that sometime during the night a particularly impassioned gust would undo his work, that I might witness the next episode. Well, we shall see. (Being married to Mr. Dickens certainly can be interesting in matters small and great.)

Monday, twenty-fifth April, aboard the Constitution, docked at Cleveland.

Thoughts of seasickness never entered my mind as we boarded this vessel early this morning at Sandusky. Seasickness was still some weeks off—when we recrossed the Atlantic. But Lake Erie thought differently. The boat rolled and tossed bringing just about all the passengers, Mr. Dickens included, into a state of abject misery. One tends to forget, at least in part, past unpleasantness, and so it was with me regarding this dreadful malady of seasickness. But now, that awaiting Atlantic crossing is painfully in my thoughts even though this ship is berthed here at Cleveland for the night. I must give Mr. Dickens credit: he is a far better traveler than I. Death at any moment was what I expected crossing Lake Erie—how could one remain alive feeling as I did. But my husband, between groans and retchings, kept repeating that this would soon be over and that one day we will look back at it all with amusement. Well, I never shall. Never!! Let the world renowned author do as he pleases.

Having decided to stay on board, I found out very little about this little city of Cleveland. But this I do know: Of the hundreds who swarmed aboard the boat to take a peek at Mr. Dickens I did not hear a single one say anything complimentary about our native land. Rather there was talk of fighting Great Britain; of bearding the British lioness (Victoria) in her den and making her howl. And amongst the hundreds who crowded aboard the boat, I did not see one who was smiling. To mention the lack of cleanliness of most and their many odours may be unkind but is entirely true. Several with particularly dirty faces, missing teeth and blood-shot eyes managed to peer into our windows much to my distress. And Mr. Dickens was so put off by everything, he actually refused to drink a toast to our Queen or to anybody else of royal blood. And he refused to receive the Mayor of Cleveland whose unkempt condition and sour expression was, at the very least, unsettling.

Before he went to sleep, after securing the curtains so no one could peer into our cabin anymore, Mr. Dickens and I spoke briefly about our impressions of these Americans of the west. That they are without exception dour, that many are boorish, that most are unfriendly, that many are dirty, odouriferous and unkempt we were in complete agreement. Culture, manners, graciousness and cleanliness ends at the Hudson River. Even New York, with all its lacks, had much to recommend it when compared to what we have experienced the past several weeks here in the west. Even the beauty of Cincinnati is only skin-deep, alas.

Wednesday, April 27, Niagara Falls, Clifton House (English side) late afternoon

I am exhausted in a way I have never experienced before. It is not physical exhaustion, nor is it mental, rather it is exhaustion of the soul. Viewing the towering magnificence of Niagara Falls transported me to a place beyond the dark side of the moon where eternity begins. I could not believe what my eyes beheld and a shudder passed through me leaving behind a searing heat which filled my throat and head causing my brains to boil—I thought my skull would explode so great was the pressure. For the first time in my life I could see myself, truly see myself. In size less than a mote of dust yet just as much a part of the whole as these falls or the entire continent of Europe. Who doubts the existence of God, let him view but a single moment this cascade and he will doubt again never. So powerful was this experience I had no eyes for Mr. Dickens or for any other human being. That he was affected, I have no doubt. But let it be his private treasure as, what happened to me is mine.

I have reread the above three times and I find the word "hyperbole" creeping into my mind. By the act of reducing what I felt to words I diminished the experience and with this diminishment comes self criticism. Perhaps it is different with Charles. Every feeling, every nuance, every mote is reduced to words by him and as he puts them down I have seen his face writhe with emotion; have seen perspiration form on his forehead, at times have seen him actually dissolve into tears with sobs so desperate he was unable to continue and must leave for one of his frantic ten mile walks. As certain as I am of anything, he will write about these falls, will write about them and write about them, each time experiencing rushes of emotion undiminished by this repetition. I have listened to him read portions of Twist and Nickleby to the children, to friends, to select audiences and every time there is anguish, joy, amusement, concern, all undiminished depending upon which portion he was reading. Yet I, by putting down several dozen words in this journal have robbed myself of the feeling that for a time transported me. Oh, what an ordinary woman I am. And how clearly I see this ordinariness being married to one of the most extraordinary human beings on earth. And, may no eyes but mine ever see this: how I hate and resent it, yet am helpless to do anything about it.

I never would have married Charles Dickens had it not been for my father. While growing up my dream was to meet and fall in love with a Cambridge man of a good county family—the son of a squire or perhaps even a knight. And the man I married would quickly rise from curate to vicar and in good time be given a deanery, possibly even that of the great Salisbury Cathedral. As wife of the dean, I would be at the center of county society and would enjoy a most comfortable and secure life surrounded by children, friends and loyal servants. If my husband was proffered a bishopric so much the better. If not, the deanery would do quite nicely. But my father was so taken with Charles: Kate, Kate, Dear Kate, he must have said a dozen times, I have the greatest expectations for Charles. He will make his mark and life with him will be most fulfilling. And I, a young, impressionable girl, who adored her father. . . .So dreams of the Cambridge man and the eventual deanery flew out the window and here I am espoused to a man who has made his mark, as my father predicted, a mark as big as Mt. Snowden. And here I am, two months away from home and missing the children so much my heart will not cease from aching. And at this moment the distant roar of the cataract is giving me a headache and I wish I had a way of turning it off.

Six hours later:

Mr. Dickens is asleep and snoring. The sound of the great waterfall lulled him and I am just as pleased to have this time to myself. I reread all I had written earlier in the day and there are several sentences I would blot out except for my original determination to let whatever I inscribed stand. And it is not only for the chance of prying eyes that I would make those deletions. I experienced embarrassment as I read these passages and am made aware what a foolish woman I can be at times. Well, here's to foolishness: in for a penny in for a pound as they say. From my earliest memory til I was about sixteen years old, the one I really wanted to marry was my father. Now, I've heard it said: little girls often want to marry their fathers. But thirteen, fourteen, fifteen even sixteen is no little girl. And it was because of this longing, impossible though it might be, that when he directed my attention to young Dickens and then continued to praise him week in and week out that my feelings finally shifted to the young man in questions. And I found myself vulnerable to his charms which were considerable, especially early on.

My mother had little use for Charles Dickens. But she never said this in so many words. Rather it was her expression every time he entered the house. Then her long silences when he was present. And ordinarily she was not one to keep silent for five minutes altogether.

I have never breathed a word of this to a living soul: but when I was about eleven and found out how absolutely impossible marriage to one's father is in this nation or, in any nation of the world, I plunged into a funk which lasted on and off, through all my adolescent years. Elements of this funk plagues me to this very day. Especially when all the family gathers for some sort of celebration. I never met a man finer than my father. I doubt if such a one exists. Not to deprecate Mr. Dickens, who of course stands head and shoulders above most men, but his teasing ways, his tenacious holding of grudges, his impatience (not with the children, certainly not with them) with me, often with his publishers, with anybody and everybody in the legal profession. . . .I could go on—all these are characteristics my father had never been burdened with. Thus Mr. Dickens tends to come up short at those times I am unable to restrain myself from comparing him to my father. With the enormity of the impact of Niagara Falls on my husband—without questions he was shaken to his foundation—nevertheless, in due course, before the day was out, he must make reference to the unfairness of the American copyright laws and how costly in pounds and shillings it had been to him personally. This to a group of Canadians who clucked in sympathy thus encouraging Mr. D. to expand on the subject for no less than fifteen minutes. That the laws are unfair is questionably true. That, in a manner of speaking, this has taken bread from the mouths of my babies is also true. But to harp on it and harp on it disregarding how offensive this might be to our American hosts and now to bring up the subject in the presence of one of the world's mightiest cataracts must be viewed, at the very least, as a character flaw—one of many I am sorry to say.

Friday, twenty-ninth April, Clifton House, Niagara Falls.

We are enjoying one of the most peaceful interludes of our American journey. Being located on the Canadian side of the Falls has shielded us from the usual hoards that beset us—Canadians are another breed altogether. When we wish to be alone (which is a good portion of the time) we have but to mention this to our kind and adoring innkeeper and the word goes out and alone we are permitted to be. In ways, the past two days have been as sweet as those during the first months of our marriage. Charles has been as attentive to me as I could wish. He has made it his business, during our rambles, to offer me his arm when the way grows even moderately uneven thus shielding me from the knocks, bruises and tumbles that ordinarily keep me black and blue. Of course there are times, as we explore the countryside, when we come across others likewise rambling, many of them recently married, Niagara Falls being a Gretna Green for lovers on this side of the Atlantic. And invariably Mr. Dickens forms instant friendships with these fellow ramblers and is not above entertaining them with bits and pieces culled from our recent travels. He is particularly fond of giving an account of our connection, or should I say lack of connection, with the Mayor of Cleveland Ohio. If I have heard this story from his lips once, I have heard it a dozen times: Mr. Dickens, having been put out by the unwelcome attention of many Clevelanders while our boat was docked at that city (they peered through our cabin windows, banged on the doors, hooted, stamped their feet, even made piercing whistles with their fingers,) he refused to leave the cabin even when called upon by the Mayor, who Mr. Dickens refused admittance despite his exalted rank. His Honor then planted himself on the wharf, directly opposite to our cabin and started to whittle, to quote Mr. D., "on a stick slightly larger than a wooden leg," and the mayor kept it up hour after hour til at last it was down, "to a small size cribbage peg." A dozen times he exploded into laughter as he gave this account of the Mayor's rather un-British behavior and a dozen times, as a dutiful wife, I joined in the laughter. But if the Mayor whittled at all, it was for ten minutes. Except for a short absence to take of some personal matters, I was planted next to the cabin window and I saw no Mayor, no whittling knife, no wooden leg sized stick. Without question, my husband's visual experiences are richer than mine. And I am not without a degree of envy. But the same story twelve times, each time with embellishments—my, oh my.

Mr. Dickens has informed me that he is going to participate in a charity performance when we reach Montreal, Canada and he bewails the fact that he has been unable to lay his hands on some of his own books. Thus he has been unable to prepare himself for certain parts he likes best. Next to eating and exercising his amorous nature, there is nothing Mr. Dickens enjoys more than putting on a skit or giving an impassioned reading from his own works. And I must say he is a skilled performer. Had he decided against a career of putting words on paper, I am certain he could have made a considerable success declaiming on stage. Perhaps even as much a success as Edmund Kean himself. Well, we will suffer through Mr. D.'s pre-performance anxiety gladly, after all it is for sweet charity and one must be charitable, mustn't one?

Wednesday, eleventh May, 1842, Montreal, Canada, Rosco's Hotel.

If there is a worse hotel anywhere in the Western Hemisphere I have not heard of it. Much to my and Mr. Dickens' surprise the hotels and inns here in Canada are generally inferior to those in that nation lying below the border. The people are so polite and accommodating, on every hand you can feel the refinement and there is so much that is British wherever you turn, that the poor condition and absolute squalor of the places of public accommodations comes as a shock. But this Rosco's Hotel, in this mostly French speaking city, is in a class by itself. Filthy! To use this word in describing conditions here is a kindness. Filth of every sort abounds. The water that flows from the taps is chocolate in colour. The bugs which inhabit the beds are not to be numbered in single or even double digits rather in legions. You hardly pay attention to the cockroaches, after all they may be disgusting but are harmless. Anyone taking a meal in the dining room is taking his life in his hands. And the smells. Yes, the putrid, cloying, sulfur smells can only be coped with by placing bits of cloves in one's handkerchief and holding it to one's nose.

Setting this leading hotel of the city aside, what has most amazed me about Montreal is that here in the heart of a British dominion the principal language spoken is French. Without French (fortunately I have enough) one is unable to get about and would be skinned alive if one chanced into one of the shops even in the better neighborhoods. Even with French the fact that we are Britishers, I am certain, adds between ten and twenty percent to any purchase, try as we may to bargain. And Mr. Dickens can be a fearsome bargainer. A beaver hat he purchased for one pound six, after thirty minutes of fierce bargaining during which he made as if to stomp out of the store, bargaining which brought this stylish piece of headware down from one pound ten, we subsequently learned from a local pharmacist, who sported an identical hat, that he had paid one pound three and had been given a brush to keep it shiny to boot. This revelation caused Mr. Dickens to go quite sour. But it was no surprise to me. I had never trusted the French, nor has a single member of my family ever since Boney and his men made a shambles of Europe.

A word of explanation as to why a gap of almost two weeks since my last entry. That I have been mildly unwell, and for sufficient reason, is only one factor. The other is that at night I have been exhausted and have gone straight to sleep as soon as I was able. And during the day there have been only brief periods when I was not tagging after Mr. Dickens, at his request, as curiosity of superhuman proportions caused him to dart in and out of places and not fail to see every sight worth seeing according to information gained from the locals as we traveled along. During the past week or two I have gained a sense that Mr. Dickens grows increasingly uneasy. That the trip we are on has begun to oppress him. And like myself, he is experiencing a terrible longing for the children. In no way is my husband the jaunty fellow he was in Boston and then in New York. And I can't help wondering if somehow he has suffered a damage, a damage to his soul as a result of this trip he so eagerly undertook. I am little changed: misery earlier, misery later. But my dear husband has gone from ebullience to a dulled reaction to most everything. Well, I hope the dramatic presentation he worked out with Lord Mulgrave will be a success and will help him out of his funk. For the past couple of days, just being with Mr. Dickens I experienced as burdensome. (Annie muttered the same thing this morning, poor thing; she is such a sensitive creature.)

Friday, thirteenth May, still at that wretched Rosco's Hotel.

I am, I am ashamed to admit, sufficiently superstitious to have awakened this morning uneasy at the prospect of Friday, the thirteenth. Contrariwise Mr. Dickens was excited at the possibility of some untoward event and declared upon leaving for the rehearsal of his play that he would seek out a black cat to cross his path and no ladder would be safe from his ducking under it and, he added, "should I spill some salt during midday meal I will refrain from tossing a pinch over my left shoulder."

Bored with shopping with dear Mr. Putnam as my companion I decided to drop into the Theatre Royal where Mr. Dickens was rehearsing. (One can do just so much shopping without everything finally becoming jumbled in one's head.) It was a delight to see Mr. D. so animated: scurrying about like a terrier you half expected to jump up into your lap and lick your cheek. The theatre is one madhouse of noise and confusion; how a presentable production will be generated out of all this defies one's imagination. But knowing my husband it will, even if he has to pull the curtains and adjust the stage lamps himself. He was very pleased to see me and between dashes here and there would throw me a kiss which made me something of a center of attraction. It took only about half a dozen blown kisses before it became generally known who I was. Then, I was the subject of kind attentions including at least half a dozen offers of tea and several plates of sweets being set around where I was sitting. I never cease to be amazed at Mr. D.'s prodigious quantity of energy. That and his capacity to work at a project unrelentingly and his remarkable critical judgement lie at the core of his genius. He has already started his book about these travels of ours. (I wonder what, if anything, he will say about me.)

Getting back to our "suite" in this hotel, Montreal's premier facility: Last night, despite the legions of voracious bugs who make our huge bed with its straw filled mattress their home, Mr. Dickens was so eager to demonstrate his amourous feeling he could not be restrained. Preparatory to this he engaged in a battle with the bugs. Gripping a fierce looking fly swatter with both hands, blood in his eye, he attacked the bugs. Now there is not a fly on earth that can resist a blow of the fearsome swatter. Not so bedbugs. They seem to just shrug off the most vicious swat, wave an antenna or two and proceed on their way. Mr. D. struck and struck. By shifting the mattress I urged the creatures out offering the coup de Grace with my scissors to those who were momentarily stunned. Perspiration standing on his brow, breathing in tight gasps, Mr. D.'s eyes had taken on their most frightening look after some forty-five minutes of this. But even with half a hundred of the little creatures gone to another life, twice that number still remained and these were the really tough ones who were no mean scurriers. What our neighbours thought of all the smacking and grunting and the occasional "gotcha" I had no way of knowing. But there were some strange looks when we both came down to breakfast. I had done a bit of killing in the morning while Mr. D. was still in bed. And he had cheered me on with: "Go get 'em, Kate, that's my girl; go get 'em, the inconsiderate creatures." Their sheer numbers had defeated his amourous intentions and I suspect, in some way, had threatened his manhood, or something of the sort. It would have all been much better before that war against the bugs began had I just feigned a headache but, and I would never admit this to Charles, he is not the only one who has amourous intentions at times.

Wednesday, twenty-fifth May, still
Rosco's Hotel, alas.

I must give thanks that Mr. Dickens chose as his primary vocation the pen rather than the stage. At least while he is engaged eight and ten hours a day at his writing table, I can get on with my tasks. And while at his writing table, unlike other authors I know, there are no rigid rules about silence and tiptoeing around while the great man disgorges the contents of his brain. In our household, if it is their wont, the children may riot with the two littlest crawling in and out of their daddy's lap with not the slightest interference in the flow of the torrent of words with which he fills quires of paper. But, as amply demonstrated the past few days and at times back home, when Mr. Dickens is engaged in a theatrical production the condition of life surrounding him can only be described as turmoil. That he emotes while washing up in the morning, at table, even when closeted in the necessarium is no more than can be expected from an intense perfectionist such as Mr. D. But his unrelenting demands for anyone and everyone to read parts, to give cues, to be totally engaged in rapt attention, added to that the turmoil that erupts when necessity draws his attention elsewhere or when some object needed for rehearsal has been misplaced, or even when the moon happens to be in the wrong portion of the sky, creates such havoc that life around him ends in a shambles and bad tempers and sharp words become the norm. So, I repeat, I give thanks that my husband, theatrically talented though he may be, only occasionally dons the thespian cloak. If it were otherwise, by now I fear I would be confined to a madhouse where I could, thankfully, find relief. All of that goes to say that the play at the Theatre Royal went off this evening to a capacity audience of many hundreds. That I had a part in the production was inevitable, although I resisted manfully up to the last possible moment. Modesty restrains me from evaluating my performance. But there was not even the hint of criticism from Mr. Dickens so one can draw one's own conclusions. Mr. D., as usual and as to be expected was magnificent. Not only did he play a variety of parts in *A Roland for Oliver, A Good Nights' Rest, and Deaf As a Post,* but he functioned as stage manager, prompter and comforter to those who were faint at heart. Lord Mulgrave was astounded at my husband's capacities, but why should he have not been? There is but one Charles Dickens—thank God. Two would put me under within a fortnight.

Early the next morning.

Need I say that Mr. Dickens was eager to celebrate in his own highly personal and inimitable fashion when we returned to our hotel after the conclusion of the play and the brief gathering afterward. But he had not reckoned with the bedbugs whose numbers, it would appear, had been replenished during the course of the day. Perhaps they had a means of communication unknown to us that alerts aunts, cousins and others that space is available. Such smashings with fly swatter, such stabbings with scissors, such scores of bugs lying dead on the carpet. Yet with every shift of the lumpy mattress more appeared; these fresh and ready for battle while we were practically on our knees from exhaustion. No need to detail the end results of our exertions. Suffice it to say Mr. Dickens slept well while I enjoyed a night of scratching and now look forward to a grumpy day. Yet I can comfort myself with the thought that a scant two weeks separates ourselves from the blessed boarding of the vessel that will take us back across the Atlantic to our home and our darling children we both so deeply miss.

Second June, 1842, Carlton House, New York

How good it is to bask in the luxury of a world class hotel—entirely bug free may I add after a diligent hunt by Mr. Dickens and myself on hands and knees, we having been rendered gun shy, so to speak, by recent experiences (Rosco's Hotel and several dreadful inns afterwards.) Mr. Dickens was growing a bit wan and avoided company and the crowds on our way down from Canada and I did my best both to comfort and protect him. In the latter Annie and dear George Putnam functioned as Pretorian guards. And how Annie enjoyed the role! But it took but several whiffs of the tainted air of New York City to restore my husband to close to his former condition. We hadn't been in the hotel half an hour when he must sally forth to a local oyster shop where he and Professor Fenton had gorged, returning an hour later so bloated with that delicacy his eyes fairly bulged from their sockets. As for me, after a good night's rest and a bath that could be recorded in the book of divine experiences (Annie kept the hot water coming til I was boiled lobster red), I was off for a wild, unrestrained bout of shopping—not a relative most distant, not a friend who had called on me at least once in the past year was to be denied an appropriate gift from the New World. Abject shame prevents me from listing the gifts I purchased for my children on the off chance that, by some misadventure, these pages are perused by eyes other than my own. Queen Victoria's dear princeling could not have fared any better if Her Majesty had taken this trip with her consort.

Early this AM, while still abed, Charles and I engaged in what can only be described as a morbid exchange. I am not certain who initiated it, perhaps it was both of us at the same moment. But within a minute or two, I was in tears and, try as he might to restrain himself, Charles broke down shortly after. In five more days we would board the packet and head East across the wide and wild Atlantic. Five short days. But what if there was another great storm? What if this time the vessel foundered and went down in the raging sea? If one pursues such morbid matters in the press, not a day passes without reports of such a tragedy taking place somewhere in the world. The sea is treacherous. Ships, no matter how sturdily built, can come apart in severe storms. Then there are shoals. Partially submerged derelicts. To say nothing of lightning strikes and winds of such ferocity nothing can stand before them. All these dreadful possibilities were offered by each of us in turn and only the force of our sobs finally choked off this exchange. Then we clung to each other, one or the other gasping out the names of our children, poor darlings, that soon might be orphans and left to shift for themselves in this cruel world. I think Mr. Dickens enjoyed the cry more than I, although it did have its soothing effects when my tear ducts finally went dry and I was able to stroke my husband's head with a series of soft: There, there, theres.

They say the bad penny always shows up. I shouldn't say this; it is not kind. And Rebecca Simmons, now Mrs. Joshua Adams, was a girlhood friend of mine. Of sorts. There was always a bit of looking down the nose at me on her part. Well, now the nose is without question on the other face—to coin a phrase.

"Oh, Kate, Kate, Kate," she said as she entered our suite, "what a delightful surprise it was to discover that you too were here in New York." I would wager my month's household allowance that she was here in the city because we were and wanted to load up with a quantity of Dickensian material and gossip to regale her envious friends back in Boston. She then turned to my poor husband, who had been furiously writing and was a bit ink spattered. "And here is the renowned Mr. Charles Dickens himself." Becky's voice went up and down the scale from what she must have fancied was the way titled English women address their equals. Then taking Charles' hand and giving it a passionate squeeze, she said, "I'm sure Kate must have told you all about our chance meeting in Boston after so many years of separation." (I had not yet introduced her and Charles looked bewildered.) But after I made the introduction, Charles, to his great credit, gave Becky's hand a vigorous shake and then in the most continental way rolled back the edge of her glove and implanted a gentlemanly kiss on her wrist. At this Becky squealed, reddened and looked pleased as Punch. Or should I say Judy in deference to her sex.

"Kate must have told you how close the two of us were during those painful years of leaving childhood behind and facing the cruelty of the world," she said still trilling up and down the scale. I had said nothing about our growing up together. In fact, other than mentioning I had met someone I knew in England years earlier, I had said nothing. Mr. Dickens at the time being busily engaged in writing a letter to Forster and clearly disinterested. "I have always liked to think that being a year older and having enjoyed more of the advantages of life than her family could afford, I was a positive influence on Kate and that the continuing loyalty of my friendship in a manner of speaking, eased the way for her when things got particularly difficult." Either she had confused me with some other unfortunate friend or was constructing this account out of the whole cloth.

"So you, are ah—is it Rebecca? Yes of course—and Kate were friends during those bygone 'painful' years." I could detect a note of amusement in Charles' voice but his face remained deadly serious. "I was not aware that she had, ah, experienced painful years and am sorry to hear it."

"Oh they were painful, Mr. Dickens. May I call you Charles?" Before he could answer she said: "Charles," brightly. "Especially for dear Kate here, Charles. Her father was an editor, you know. And you know how impoverished those connected with magazines and newspapers tend to be. Yet those of the press declare themselves gentlemen and are forced to struggle, and this is the tragedy, struggle manfully to maintain at least the appearance of gentlemen, often at a severe sacrifice to their families."

More often than not my father went threadbare so his family could be respectably clothed. And I doubt if even once in his life he thought of himself as a gentleman. Gentlemen did not regularly come home with printer's ink on their hands, and certainly did not sleep over in their shop in order to make a publication date.

"Considering how difficult things were for her," Becky went on, "I was dumbstruck when I heard what a fortunate marriage she had made. Yes dumbstruck, Charles. And at the same time so happy for her. And yes, even a tiny bit jealous. Don't dare breathe a word of that to Mr. Adams. He dotes on me, you know. The dear, sweet man."

"Oh rest assured, dear lady, my lips are sealed." Charles pinched his lips together and I believe I detected a quick wink. "The Grand Inquisitor himself could not bring me to utter a single word employing his utmost torture." Becky looked pleased. Then she took in one of those deep breaths of hers and held it for several moments.

"Mr. Adam and I have been planning a trip to England," she said coyly. "I have pressed him for half a dozen years and finally he agreed. Wouldn't it be just wonderful if he and I and you and Kate could meet and then, as old friends are wont to do, ramble through the countryside where we grew up and talk about times long ago."

"Oh yes, such a ramble would be wonderful," said Charles shooting his cuffs. "But your mentioning that reminded me that His Honour, the Mayor of New York, has asked me to take a ramble with him through the Battery and I must be off." With that, popping his hat on his head and bowing to Becky, he was out the door and I could hear him whistling down the hallway That his destination was the oyster bar I had no doubt. And I couldn't help remembering that upon returning to our suite with Professor Fenton one time, he had proudly announced he had consumed three dozen blue point oysters. I wondered if he would attempt to match or even exceed that number this time. If ever Mr. Dickens is reincarnated it will be as a starfish. Smile! What a thing to say.

Becky Simmons aside, and it is my fervent wish she remain so—the thought of her coming to England causes shudders to run up and down my spine—it has been exciting to see Mr. Dickens ply his pen six or seven hours at a time as he has been doing the past several days. Suffering from a sore throat, his surgical scar causing short bouts of stabbing pain, have slowed him scarcely at all, his daily production of what will be his American notes exceeds eight pages.

Fourth June, 1842, Tarrytown.
Mr. Washington Irving's Country

We have managed to travel the beautiful Hudson River Valley, if not incognito at least with a minimum of fanfare. These displaced Dutch burghers are a dour lot. And although they will come out to stare, not even the youngest will venture closer than a rod and there are no pleas for locks of hair, autographs or even handshakes. For me this highly restrained reception during our final short excursion in America has been a most welcome relief. For Mr.

Dickens, after the first day I could detect a slight malaise as if this coolness somehow nullifies the previous months of unrestrained enthusiasm. It would appear that adulation is a sort of opiate for Mr. Dickens, the withholding of which brings on poorly concealed uneasiness which translates into irritability when we are alone together. If he should ever fall out of fashion, which has been the fate of so many other authors, I fear that his suffering might increase to the point that life itself becomes intolerable. Well, if such a manifestation of the public's fickleness ever takes place, I will do all I can to solace the poor man and my loyalty shall be unwavering.

As we ramble this most English of countrysides (absent the Catskills of course) as might be expected Mr. Dickens is never without a book of Washington Irving's into which he thrusts his nose every time we stop for refreshment at one of the rough-hewn local inns. He takes particular delight in identifying locales mentioned in the book and will ask any local inhabitants he happens to meet a score of questions, not pausing for an answer before plunging in with the next question. Meeting with dear Mr. Irving and being escorted through Sleepy Hollow was, without question, the high point of this excursion for Mr. Dickens. I was less impressed. After all, one place is very much like another and, I must confess, I do not revere literature. But I was delighted by Mr. Dickens' offerings of sugar suspended by a string that various tea drinkers seated around a large table took sucks on followed by sips of tea, I really was tickled having read about that old custom in one of Mr. Irving's stories. Not sanitary, perhaps, but so unique. I even had thoughts of preparing such a lump upon my return to England and trying it on various of our friends.

There are times when my husband's amorous needs get the best of me. The past two days have been robbed of a portion of their beauty and pleasure because of his twice, even thrice daily insistence, only some of which I can resist. Knowing my wifely duties tempers my resistance.

Although half a year away from Halloween, last night Mr. Dickens somehow got hold of a large pumpkin which he proceeded to carve into a fierce creature—one that would stop your heart had you chanced upon it at night on a lonely road. To test the efficacy of this creation, under the influence of *The Legend of Sleepy Hollow*, he hired a spirited horse, the blackest one in the livery stable, then borrowing some bits and pieces from our inn keeper he dressed himself in black and, placing a lighted candle inside the pumpkin went out on the road. Three times I saw him galloping madly by, pumpkin on the pomerel, his greatcoat streaming out behind him. He may have terrified a toddler or two. But the Dutch who came to their windows as he dashed by only shook their heads. It would appear that they are well read as far as the works of Washington Irving are concerned. But finally, when he heaved the pumpkin over a fence, his night ride having come to an end, the farmer whose land it was came to the door of his house and shook his fist at Mr. Dickens. Had it not been for that shook fist Mr. Dickens might have deemed his night ride a failure. But having a fist shook at one, especially if that one has known so much adulation, tickled his funny bone and he came back into our inn in high spirits. "So what do you think of Ichabod Crane," he said laughing. I was tempted to correct him. It was a chap named Broome who made the ride. But knowing how little my dear husband likes correction I forebear. But later when he was busily engaged in his American notes, I placed a copy of Mr. Irving's works, opened to the proper page, where Mr. Dickens' eyes could not fail to fall upon it.

Can one be actually hungry for one's children? I want to consume them in a way only a mother can. I want to hug all four of them at once and hug them and hug them. A short while ago I told Mr. Dickens of this hunger and he grunted. I'm not certain if he heard me or not, so deeply involved was he is his project. Although there is no better father than my husband, I know that in ways he is incapable of loving our four darlings as deeply as I. If I dared say this to him, woe betide me. He would flare up and unleash a torrent of words that would leave me prostrated. But to me my children are everything. There is nothing in the world that even comes close in importance. But with Mr. Dickens, who can doubt that it is otherwise? Knowing of this involvement with my children provides me with a sense of comfort, of satisfaction also. Outside of the home I am as an ant compared to a lion which is Mr. Dickens. But within the home things are quite different. And say what you may, inside one's home is more important than outside. As they say: the child is father of the man. And we women are the ones who raise and most influence these little fathers. When I finally cross the threshold of Devonshire Terrace, less than a month hence, I doubt if I will emerge for any reason for at least a quarter of a year. I have a lot of mothering to catch up with. Oh, to feel the sheltering walls of my home surrounding me again! I'm coming home, dear children, Mother is coming home.

Tenth June, 1842, aboard the George Washington.

I cannot give too much praise to my dear husband for choosing this sailing ship for our return voyage rather than another steam packet. This ship fairly dances over the swells and troughs; there is no more fearsome belching of sparks and smoke from chimneys that look as if they were fashioned in Dante's underworld. No more odour from burning coal, no more head splitting throb, throb, throb from the infernal engine. What a relief! Three days at sea and neither Mr. Dickens nor I have suffered a bout of sea-sickness. Alas, not so for some of our fellow passengers. But they were not hardened to the extremes of ocean travel as were Mr. Dickens and I. Speaking of Mr. D., the dear man, he has located several companions who have formed a maniacal association (Mr. Dickens' words) named the United Vagabonds. They troop from one end of the ship to the other cutting up with Mr. D. playing the accordion furiously, another at the violin, yet another tooting the key bugle. This medley goes on at all hours of the day and night, each musician rendering his own unique music and, trooping behind them, a grin from ear to ear, is the black steward who has renounced his duties for the company of these madcaps. The captain of this ship having fallen sick, Mr. Dickens has determined to cure him and has so announced to crew and passengers hinting that at one time he was trained as a doctor's assistant. I dare not betray even a hint that his entire contact with the medical profession has been as a suffering subject of their none too gentle ministrations lest Mr. Dickens fly into mock fury and embarrass me to tears. (I am grown quite fragile emotionally as with the passing of each day we grow closer to home.) As far as Mr. Dickens' medical skills are concerned, the ship's Captain's miraculous recovery or his continued distress will ultimately be the proof. At this point nothing about Mr. Dickens— word or deed—surprises me. Thus I am prepared for the poor captain to bound from his bed fully restored or, God forbid, expire in the course of the next forty-eight hours. I truly believe if Mr. Dickens declared he had found a method of traveling to the moon and for me to start packing, I would only shrug and begin selecting garments suitable for the climate on that heavenly body. That Mr. Dickens has me pretty well bamboozled, as the Americans say, is quite evident. I defy anyone to be in the company of this human Mt. Vesuvius as much as I and not end up thoroughly bamboozled. Where does he get his energy??!! They say there is no one with greater energy than a toddling two year old, that any adult trying to keep up with one would collapse of exhaustion within an hour. Well, let that two year old try and keep up with Mr. D.—Let the British isles champion prize fighter try and keep up with him on one of his ten mile walks that have been described as being like that of the Furies.

Now Mr. Dickens has hinted he would like me to join him in one of his readings; that the passengers expect him to give at least one. And that he is considering two or three to ease the boredom of this oceanic passage. I will find a way to refuse even if it requires that I develop an appropriate indisposition due to the delicate condition I believe I am in. It will take me the full three weeks of our passage to recover from the physical and emotional exhaustion of our trip. Preparing for and delivering a reading would prostrate me. So Mr. D. will have to go it alone, which he, of all people, is fully capable of doing. As I write these words here come the United Vagabonds with their ear-splitting cacophony. That it lacks an hour and ten minutes to midnight seems to make no difference to these "merrymakers." If it were anyone but Mr. Charles Dickens in the lead, I am certain that lots would be drawn amongst the passengers to determine who would be the one to throw these instrumentalists overboard. But Mr. Dickens is so beloved, worshipped might be the more accurate word, that even the most dyspeptic old grizzly on board can be seen grinning as this band marches by. Yet the ill ship's captain is another matter. If Mr. Dickens fails in his medical attempts, that old sea dog may decide to clap my husband in irons for the remainder of the voyage. And aboard ship the captain's word is law without any chance of appeal! Mr. Dickens clapped in irons would be quite a sight, would it not. Restrain all that energy! My God, he and the ship along with him might explode.

Twelfth June, 1842, the George Washington, Atlantic Ocean.

Charles Dickens triumphs, Kate Dickens fails abysmally. Oh well, what can one expect when you place the timid little field mouse alongside the trumpeting Indian elephant? From his medicine chest Mr. Dickens solemnly produced a variety of nostrums for the poor captain's benefit. Pills and plasters, bitter droughts and noxious purges and at sunrise this morning the ship's commander was up and about singing the praises of Mr. Dickens between bellowed orders to the crew whose movements bounded from slow trots to vigorous gallops under the lashing of his tongue assisted by indiscriminately offered kicks and blows as he prowled the decks of the vessel. Even the breeze freshened and the ship plunged forward with renewed vigour as if whoever it is who controls the wind was cowed by the recovered captain's tantrum. As one might expect, my husband pranced discreetly behind the captain, grinning and gesturing lest even one of the passengers be not fully aware of his role in the miraculous cure. That Mr. Dickens' reading from The Old Curiosity Shop that evening was also triumphant, attended by mighty roars of applause, only served to make my failure more abysmal. Overcoming all my objections, pounding at me with a torrent of words til my backbone fairly turned to jelly, Mr. Dickens secured my cooperation— little Nell was to be my bête noire. (Thousands, nay tens of thousands of Englishmen would attack me with their fists if it became known that I characterize their dear, desperate, desolate Little Nell in this fashion.) I made a stink of the whole affair. I lost my place half a dozen times. I misread, inserting words of my own—a desecration that causes the world-renowned author to become apoplectic. I giggled in the most inappropriate places. And to cap it all, I tripped and fell while attempting an exit when the reading was over. When Mr. Dickens returned to our cabin he said nothing: only glared and made a sound in his nose. Then turning his back to me, after a single humph, he was asleep and snoring within moments.

I guess it was that humph, followed by those snores, that finally cast an amusing light on the entire affair. That I would not be called upon to participate in another reading during the remainder of our journey I was certain. And should Mr. Dickens' distaste for my histrionic abilities continue after we are once again comfortably situated at Devonshire Terrace, one thing is certain: I will not be broken hearted. Despite a rather credible performance back in Montreal, I am no actor. My skills are confined to my role as wife and mother and mistress of our household. Would that Mr. Dickens accepted that—being wed to such a man is demanding enough.

After that dramatic fiasco, I do not know if I dare show my face for the rest of the trip. Embarrassment, chagrin and finally despair were my portions earlier this evening. If not for the children I might even have thrown myself overboard and ended it all. For I have this foreboding that the path that lies ahead of me will be rockstrewn and filled with increasing numbers of thorns, brambles and ultimately volcanic ash. Living in the shadow of Mt. Vesuvius, one cannot escape unscathed.

Thirteenth June, the George Washington, Atlantic Ocean

My wounds of last night are, if not healed, at least partially so. Fortunately, without exception the passengers aboard this vessel are both kind and considerate. In their kindness they have converted a fiasco into a comic interlude and I have been praised and petted til I have come close to believing what they say; close but not completely. And there is still a residue of embarrassment.

If I did not know him as well as I do, I would begin to suspect that Mr. Charles Dickens has taken leave of his senses and is headed in the direction of the madhouse. He cavorts like a six year old child. From morning til night he is engaged in pranks irrespective of the victims' age, sex, or condition. But his popularity is such that even the use of an India rubber device that when placed beneath the cushion of a chair and sat upon gives forth an unmentionable sound elicits only a good-natured laugh from various ones who, under different circumstances, might even resort to administering a drubbing to the trickster with their walking sticks. The children, and there are a baker's dozen of them, idolize him. And why should they not? He gets down on his hands and knees without regard to who may be watching and plays horsey, catch the bear, leap frog and games of his own invention. Seeing him cavorting with them causes a constriction of my heart as I think of my own poor babies yet many days away from my embrace and doubtless pining for me and moping about this very moment. I try not to be resentful of Mr. Dickens' attention to these children of strangers. But resentment does creep in and I end up feeling ashamed of myself. And if ever there was evidence of a charter defect. This reaction of mine surely is one. I shall try to improve. This sort of reaction is not worthy of Mr. Hogarth's daughter and diminishes me as a person.

Fourteenth June, 1842, still aboard the George Washington.

I have been struck down by a bout of seasickness whose severity for several hours, was such that I did not care if I lived or died. Although, to a degree, solicitous I sensed that Mr. Dickens viewed me as weak—as if it were my fault—I could see it in his expression and the way he jauntily bounced around as if to mock me. But within an hour the bouncing and mocking had come to an end as he too was as closely engaged with the slop bucket as was I. Except when he suffered that operation to his fistula, I have never seen him in such a desperate state. "I am going to die, Kate," he moaned, his face growing paler by the moment. "Take good care of the children and do the best you can with my manuscripts and other writings so that each of them may have a modest patrimony when they come of age." That he was not going to die I was certain. And I confess I did not experience much in the way of compassion. And when the howling in the cabin reached a crescendo I staggered out of doors to gain a few moments of relief. Yet conscience, that peculiar sprite whose caress is always with a pitchfork, so prodded me that after a few breaths of fresh air I staggered back into the cabin to tend to the "dying" man who, to my relief, was sound asleep, one arm cradling his head while his other hand rested on his face just like little Charlie when he is fast asleep. I couldn't help being struck how youthful Mr. Dickens appeared—sleep having smoothed his forehead and banished the crows' feet from the corners of his eyes. It is easy to lose awareness that he has not yet reached the halfway mark in his allotted three score and ten—that in the way of the world he is still a rather young man despite accolades as the lion of literature. Encased in all that remarkable genius is a core of boyishness: eager for attention, unsure at times, often afraid, constantly needing comforting. It is at times like this that I am able to reassure myself how essential I am to his well-being, how desperate would be his condition if fate caused me to be his constant companion, wife and loyal friend no longer.

Fifteenth June, the George Washington, almost halfway back to England!!!

Well, well, and a few more wells, how remarkably my dear husband has recovered from his near brush with "death." If my condition were not already delicate, the proofs of affection he has bestowed upon me these past half a dozen hours would guarantee that it would be. At the moment he is writing like a fury, chuckling over some American incident that within a month or two will amuse loyal readers the length and breadth of the British Isles. Earlier, as we dined, I heard some mutterings from him regarding copyright laws, his pet peeve. If he insists on including this in his forthcoming "American Notes," it will cost him thousands of readers—most of the American newspapers have already roundly condemned him for his "petulant" attitude. Yet, since his rewards for his efforts on the western shores of the Atlantic continue not to be financial, it is possible he does not give a tinker's damn if he loses American readers or not. I, for one, should be glad if all his future writings were kept out of the hands of those New World literary pirates. And I would support hanging as a penalty for this sort of piracy as it is for those outlaws who seize ships. Well, Kate Hogarth Dickens, you are the bloodthirsty one! Yet I will offer no defense other than every volume of Mr. Dickens' works pirated steals a portion from his children rightfully theirs. So hang them and I will not shed a tear! On a less bloodthirsty note, I cannot help wondering if Mr. Dickens plans to include some references to his long-suffering wife in the volume he is working on. Vanity, vanity, all is vanity as the Bible says (exactly who I don't quite remember, maybe Solomon.) It would be nice, after I am dead and gone, to have my name preserved in print for those who come after and might wonder about their great, great grandmother. Well, at least there still are those portraits by Maclise and you hear more and more about the method, using chemicals, of creating a likeness developed by that fellow Daguerre, the Frenchman. If I am assured it is not dangerous perhaps such a likeness, surrounded by my dear children, could be obtained. But not until after the baby is born. Why my face insists upon swelling the way it does. . . .

Twentieth June—a scant week from sighting land, so the captain tells us.

I am grown weary: of this seemingly endless ocean voyage; of Mr. Dickens cavorting when he is not furiously writing; of the tiresome adulation of our fellow passengers; of life. Samuel Johnson once said: when one grows tired of London one is tired of life. Well, the George Washington is my London and the ocean, as it laps against the sides of this vessel, tempts me to take the two or three extra steps and then over the rail and into its welcoming bosom. If not for my babies, who await the return of their too-long absent mother. . . .What a bitter thing is melancholia! Mr. Dickens, who would scoff at the suggestions that he is subject to attacks of this sickness of the soul, has his own unique way of fending it off. Or should I say of constructing an armour of his own manufacture so that his soul is not torn so often as is the case with his poor wife who cowers helplessly when this dark malady strikes. What is the armour that Mr. Dickens employs? He attempts and often succeeds in out-doing that disease. Such was the case earlier this evening.

I was beginning to see a hollowness in his cavorting, a tightening of his features, an impatience he tried to conceal but was revealed by the set of his jaw and the abruptness of his response when approached by the steward or other members of the crew, thus I was not at all surprised when he announced to our fellow passengers at the midday meal that he would be pleased to entertain them with a reading at tea time. To this announcement came shouts, blown kiss-es and a burst of applause. Then when I saw him taking up a copy of Oliver Twist and thumbing through its pages, I knew with absolute certainly which passages he would choose. Of course I had seen all of this before. But when he transformed himself into a demonic being, fire flashing from his eyes, every nerve and muscle in his body vibrating, his voice the very echo of doom as he thundered that por-tion recounting the murder of Nancy by Sykes leading to Sykes' death, for the moment my depression was swept away as my blood ran cold at the horror of what I was hear-ing. And horror was reflected in the faces of the scores gath-ered on deck as the sun was sinking below the horizon. No melancholia, no matter how bitter its generative force, could match the emotions Mr. Dickens' reading generated. Two women fainted. Tears streamed from eyes, male and female. Handkerchiefs were in constant use for eyes, nose. Perspiration covered foreheads. Back in our cabin, after he had fairly devastated the George Washington's entire complement of passengers, red-eyes, drenched with perspiration, Mr. Dickens performed a crazy dance, snapping his fingers and puffing his lips, while partially suppressed squeals of laughter escaped his throat. Once again he had conquered his melancholia in his own inimitable fashion. Alas, within the hour my depression returned and pressed down on my shoulders like Jeremiah's yoke. While Mr. Dickens, his face cherubic, almost childlike in its smoothness, lies peacefully sleeping to awake in the morning almost certainly in high spirits to lead the United Vagabonds through another day of discordant concerts and good natured mischief.

Twenty-fifth June, two, no more than three days from Devonshire Terrace.

This is the third time I have picked up my journal then put it down without inscribing a word since my last entry. Til this morning my body felt as if it were encased in lead. It was all I could do to draw in a breath then let it out again.

Not a morsel of food passed my lips in seventy-two hours, only sips of water which brought with them waves of nausea. But this was not seasickness. Rather a melancholia of such proportions the only thing I could think of was the graveyard: the idea of my body being consigned to the sea keeping me alive. The cold sea with its fishes tearing away mouthfuls of my flesh—anything but that. But upon opening my eyes this morning and realizing that our voyage was so close to its termination, as if by a miracle, every trace of distress was gone and such pangs of hunger—the stewards stared at me in amazement and I have seldom seen Charles look as pleased. The poor man really has been under a burden the past few days and I must say, no husband could have been kinder or more thoughtful. That part of his concern was due to my delicate condition is certainly understandable. I believe he has already fallen in love with the little one. But most of his concern was for me and there were hours altogether when he sat alongside and held my hand allowing some of his strength to flow into me.

Friday evening, first July, 1842, Home! Home! Home!

What can I say now that I am returned to Devonshire Terrace and in the bosom of my family. I shudder as I record here that upon our entering the door of this dear house Charlie was so emotionally overwhelmed at the sight of his papa and mama that he fell into convulsions and until Dr. Elliotson could be summoned my husband and I feared for the life of the child, so violent were the convulsions, so ghastly pale his face, so frail his appearance as we did everything in our power to comfort him and prevent him from injuring himself. The doctor was amazed at the child's reaction, saying he had never witnessed the like in an otherwise perfectly healthy boy. That this incident and all the excitement of our homecoming left me completely drained so that I shortly had to take to my bed was no more than any normal human being might expect. But Mr. Dickens is no normal human being. Once it was established that Charlie was in no danger and after an hour's wild romp with the other children, he was off to Macready in Clarence Terrace and to who knows where else, energy fairly pouring from him like steam from a locomotive engine. Other than that incident with Charlie, all is well here at Devonshire Terrace. And, as far as I can ascertain, amongst our friends and other family members. For that I think God and will continue to offer thanks to the Author of Creation each and every day.

I can feel my cheeks redden with a sort of embarrassment as I start to put the following words down: Although glad to be home and, of course thankful, I am not as filled with joy as I expected to be. In fact at odd times there is a heaviness and a feeling of malaise against which I must exercise all my ability so as not to reveal it. As the George Washington got closer and closer to England there was such an upsurge of expectation, such excitement. Then when we passed Cape Clear and sailed along the coast of Ireland every nerve in my body tingled. Need I say how wild was the cheering when we sighted the light at Holyhead. And then by morning Liverpool with a grand farewell breakfast and such huggings and slaps on the back and declarations of undying friendship as was never before seen on earth. Then tearing southward by train through England's glorious green countryside, counting the minutes, my heart racing so I found it difficult to breathe. And now—and now it, everything, is back to normal and I can feel a dullness creeping in. As expected, and I would not have it any other way, I am back in the routine of everyday living: Running the house. Dealing with the servants and tradesmen. Binding and kissing the little hurts of the children. Protecting the younger ones from the jabs and kicks of the older while trying to sort out the muddle of our finances after months of neglect. But to the question: Would I ever again embark on such a journey with Mr. Dickens? The answer is an emphatic no. Give me a week or two and this malaise, this feeling of dissatisfaction will pass and I will truly settle into the bosom of my family.

Only a few pages left in my precious journal. Now the question is: what to do with it so that its contents are protected from prying eyes—woe betide me should some of the things I penned in these pages be revealed. Perhaps it would be best if I consigned it to the hearth fire. That would end any possibility of mischance. But the thought of allowing these dear pages to be consumed, leaving only ashes behind causes a constriction of my heart???? I shall place them in the hands of the Reverend David Davies, free thinker and independent soul that he is. Let him find a secure place for this journal in his little chapel out amidst the downs of Surrey to be kept safe and secure til I and, yes, my children have departed this earth for a better life. Then what matter whose eyes peruse these then yellowed and brittle pages? Who will even remember Kate Dickens a hundred years hence?

Sunday, third of July 1842.

This time, without embarrassment, I can say I am fairly riddled with dissatisfaction and have been acting the bear to everyone but my children, with an occasional lapse when all four of them are going at it at once. That a portion of this dissatisfaction flows from resentment at the mountains of attention being bestowed on Mr. Charles Dickens cannot be denied. King Charles II, on his return to England, could have scarcely been received with more accolades. The newspapers are full of "Mr. Dickens, Mr. Dickens, Mr. Dickens." While I am arguing with the greengrocer, paying off the butcher, comforting Annie who has been in a state of constant weeping since our return and, of course, being a doting mother to four children who must have fancied themselves orphans for the five months we were gone. Not that people are not happy to see me. Good old Kate; steady, completely reliable Kate; always a comfort to her husband, why should they not be happy to see me? But had I, through mischance, failed to return, who other than my precious children would have been distraught. Yet had Mr. Dickens found his grave in the New World, all of England would have gone into mourning, such is the enthusiasm of the reception at his return. I don't know what sort of a person this makes me (and I'm not sure I care) but I take comfort from the thought that "it," all if "it," cannot last. The time will come, surely within the next decade, when his popularity will fade and attention and affection of the public will be directed elsewhere. Look how the reputation of Jane Austin has begun to fade. For my taste she was a more accomplished author than Mr. Charles Dickens. Nothing he was written, not even Pickwick, has delighted me as much as *Pride and Prejudice*. But the public is fickle and poor Jane Austin is going out of style and in time will be scarcely read. And so it undoubtedly will be with the man I married. Give it another ten years—he will be scarcely forty, still a youngish man—and like my father he will likely be editing some respected publication and our life together will have settled down to some degree of normalcy. My intuition tells me that five will be the number of children in our family and that Mr. Dickens and I will move gracefully into our later years, enjoying an increasing degree of privacy and we will look back at these frantic years with amusement, our chief satisfaction being the affection and accomplishments of our children and our love for one another.

And so Catherine Dickens' journal ends.

Editor's note: In all, Kate Dickens bore her husband ten children. In 1858 Dickens separated from his wife and sent her away. Then he established an intimate relationship with the actress Ellen Ternan while Catherine's younger sister, Georgiana, continued to supervise the affairs of the Dickens' household.